The Tide Turns

Hal Alpiar

©2025 Nightengale Press
A Division of Nightengale Entertainment LLC

THE TIDE TURNS

For information about Nightengale Press
please visit our website at www.NightengaleEntertainment.com.
Email: publisher@nightengalepress.com

Alpiar, Hal,
THE TIDE TURNS/ Hal Alpiar
ISBN 13: 978-1-947257-50-6
Fiction

First Published by Nightengale Press in the USA

September 2025

10 9 8 7 6 5 4 3 2 1

Printed in the USA

DEDICATION

Special thanks to my editor and publisher, Valerie Martin, to my brother, Rick Alpiar and his wife Anne, to my daughter, Haley Murphy, to my son, Christopher Alpiar, and to my institutionalized daughter, Melissa Alpiar.

Also thanks to my friends, Rob Boyd, Carol Kirsimagi, and her son, John Kirsimagi, and Susan Moore Bray Franks.

The Tide Turns

Chapter 1

Sorting out, sort of...

Saturday morning. Pillows, peanuts, magazines. Reading the barf bags. And never a drop spills during their first-class champagne flight from New Jersey's Newark Airport.

A smooth landing. They step onto the tarmac. Like a sauna with a fan. They tug their wide-brimmed hats and even with sunglasses, still need to squint.

Each has a backpack slung over one shoulder. They work their way past the primitive airport's baggage area to the entrance. An old, open-top, mud-covered Jeep awaits them at the curb. It could have been green once. Or blue. Names. Smiles. Handshakes. Strap in the backpacks. They climb aboard.

Ten minutes out, hugging the rollbar, they hurtle up and down lane and a half wide Costa Rican mountain roads, kicking up clanging stones and thick unbreathable dirt clouds. The white-knuckle ride leaves little room to enjoy the tropic lushness, or beautiful paths strewn with machete-cut vines and palm leaves, especially when trying to pass an oncoming truck at three miles per hour with a sharp quarter-mile cliff at the road's edge. Both vehicles need to back up to go forward.

Their driver jabbers incoherently nonstop as they catapult over potholes big enough to hold a dead refrigerator—or tourist. The cheap bubbly airline Brut regurgitates up enough to taste foul and feel like it's floating their back teeth.

A bone-rattling hour later, sand kicks up with great exuberance in an abrupt skidding halt in front of the remote Playa Rica Oceanfront Resort. They detach themselves from the rollbar and exhale in tandem. But even before they can fully collect their stomachs, they're greeted by toothy smiles, a plunking guitar and giant complimentary welcome drinks.

On wobbly legs, they sip and laugh politely before stumbling behind their luggage boys to an isolated beach cottage and—without even unpacking or opening a drawer—they plunk down their welcome drinks, collapse onto the bed and sleep until dark creeps along the sand. Two hours pass. They awake abruptly to light tapping sounds.

He rubs his eyes and rises. She sits up. He crosses the room, peeks out the window, then smiles as he flips on the light and turns to throw open the door.

They grin nonstop at the gastronomic entourage of festively-dressed employees carrying in all the makings of what looks like a knock-out meal for ten. But it's served instead to just the two of them, by candlelight, with soft guitar and rum punch accompaniment.

With barely a crumb left on their plates, the staff and guitarist nod, smile and quietly depart, leaving them to fresh fruit dessert and a shimmering sunset over the ocean.

They dabble in the dessert, then exit the cottage and stroll down the empty beach, hand-in-hand, to the Pacific's low-tide edge. He spots a large abandoned towel and shakes off the sand. They sit and stare numbly at a hundred incoming waves before turning to face each other and make love by patchy moonlight. They stand to kiss again and return to their room.

Sunday. Unexpected grins. Nods. Handshakes and back pats all around as they try unsuccessfully to tiptoe unnoticed for a curious look see into a small Southern Baptist Church service on the beach a few hundred yards south of their resort. A "God's Not Dumb" sermon is followed by blessings all around. Then pineapple cake. A picked-this-mornin' cup of coffee and chitchat with the two-dozen faithful. Then a glorious sun and surf all-day walk on powder white sand, rewarded with drinks and seafood on the beach.

Monday is literally consumed with beach, ocean kayaks, native handmade arts and crafts, souvenir shop stops, and snorkeling. The fresh fish and vegetables dinner cooked over a bonfire is brought to their linen-covered table anchored in the sand in ankle-deep warm water at the edge of the cove. Candlelight. White wine. Cloth napkins. Bottomless rum cocktails. Wet feet and rolled-up cuffs.

Feeling like they've hit the lottery, it's their first—and perhaps, each thinks, their last—splurge with the reward money for helping capture the now famous Mafia mobster, Apple Solamenté.

Tuesday. After a late breakfast, they meander over to the poolside Bamboo Bar with concrete stools built into the pool floor on one side of the bar with seats that are two to three inches below the water level. The seating arrangement is so that you can get drunk and just fall in. After a moment of smiling and considering the options, JP and Maddigan decide to commandeer a dry, raised level corner next to the pool on the patio side.

"Hey, Professor, you know what?" Underpinning JP's voice is an almost inaudible giggle. "Now that our meltdowns are definitely over, maybe we should think about staying here awhile? Costa Rica looks pretty nice, y'know?" She sweeps an arm at the blanket of bursting hibiscus surrounding the property.

"Like more swimming and sailing and snorkeling and hiking and more, uh, you know—other stuff." Twisting the fine, black shoulder-length hair behind her left ear, her grin triggers her dimple. "Oh, yeah, and—"

"Exotic drinks?" He laughs as he sits back on his sweeping ocean view bamboo barstool and toasts her with his icy rum drink.

"Well, that's cool, Rick. Slushy, even," she quips. "Maybe you're gettin' brain freeze with all that crushed ice you've got, but Frozen Coco-Loco's are not exactly what's on my fuzzy little brain."

"Just because you're only five-two, who says your brain is little, JP?" In the middle of his barn-red sunburn and scruffy whiskers, his cheeks lift his grin to a smile. His white teeth dance to her attention. "Oh, and about it being Fuzzy, well…."

She whispers, "Yeah, right! Thanks, big five-ten Professor. But not so fuzzy that it didn't get us out of major trouble and earn us the money to cover this vacation, and…."

"Okay, okay. I give. You're right about the trouble, and besides, I know what's really on your mind, young lady!"

"So, when'd you start being a psychic, old man?" She pauses then looks around before responding. "'Cuz, you are right this time, Rick, except for maybe the 'lady' part." Still grinning, she stays with the thought, rolling her narrow green eyes, "and as for the young part you mentioned, by the way, maybe I could take a couple of years off of your hide after this drink and a little swim?"

"We gotta swim?" He deadpans as he swishes the straw around in his drink, plowing swirls through the crushed ice.

"Sure. Swims are good. Gives us, y'know, the chance to start out, uh, well, you know—wet!" She's grinning now, ear to ear. He gets her message, but motions to the drink that he wants to finish it first.

"What's to rush?" he says. "We're on vacation, right?" She nods, scans the horizon and returns to face Maddigan.

"Okay," she says, "so—once we're done playing Costa Rican Rendezvous, I think—and I've been thinking about this, Rick—maybe we should—seriously—start to live more frugally, like we used to?" JP raises one eyebrow as if to underscore that her statement is a question, then continues, "Y'think you can be frugal?" Her other eyebrow joins in shifting to an air of expectancy, "Y'think you can resist the urge to splash the money around?"

He sips. He squints. "Frugal," he repeats like he's reading from a phone book.

A soaring frigate and two gulls swoop playfully above the row of breakwater rocks. The sun is scorching, but offshore breezes and icy rum drinks override any thoughts of needing sunburn cream. A few puffball clouds float in the clear blue sky above the periodic whitecaps that dot the rolling waves.

He breaks into whispering words to a song with a little shimmy move thrown in. "Splash the money around, JP? As in—

Splish, Splash,
I was takin' a bath,
long about Saturday night.
Rub dub, I was splashing in the tub,
thinkin' everything was all right

and then?"

Hands on hips, she flashes her dimple. Maddigan grins back. He laughs out loud. Their exchange turns heads as he hums more and dances, then sprawls uninhibitedly atop a high stool.

Clearly preoccupied with sloshing his Coco-Loco concoction around inside his coconut shell and admiring the leavings of JP's string bikini, he is paying no attention to anyone besides her.

"Yeah, that's me, Green Eyes, good old Professor Frugal!"

Both are aware that they've aged mentally and emotionally—and added a few gray hairs—after their brutal run-in with Apple Solamenté and his gangster crime family. The boat-sinking. The

11

murders. The drug-deal adventure. All were capped by an old-fashioned movie scene shoot-out, except it wasn't a movie. And both admitted it "Scared the shit outta us!"

In the middle of the gunshots, blood and dead bodies, "Old Man Apple" ended up in federal prison for the rest of his life. Maddigan and JP escaped with some aches, pains, scratches, and the equivalent of war zone post-traumatic stress syndrome.

Of course, the professor and his prize student won major media attention they never imagined. The huge, unexpected amount of reward money—for inadvertently sabotaging the Solamenté Mob's demise under JP's intuitive strategizing—was at the same time staggering and problematical. The ten percent of recovered drug exchange cash reward—$1,250,000 to be exact non-taxable—was split fifty-fifty with $625,000 deposited into each of their near bankrupt accounts.

The sudden windfall should more than make up for their unwanted fifteen minutes of fame, shouting reporters thrusting microphones and flashbulb bombardments in their faces. But the sudden accumulation of wealth presented yet another round of shock waves they never imagined. Day-after-day onslaughts of hungry lawyers, financial advisors, investment groups, charity fundraisers, shysters, and struggling business startups, filled their mailbox, voicemail, and pounded-down sand driveway.

They disconnected the doorbell, strung a chain across the hard-sand driveway, kept the blinds closed, and turned off the phone ringer. All they knew for sure was that they needed a quick vacation to step back, rest, relax, and sort things out. They decided to start at Newark Airport. And now they're here in Guanacaste, Costa Rica with murderer Mafioso gangster Apple Solamenté—pronounced "Sola'men'tay—now serving life in prison. They are all about needing to begin anew, happily, and hopefully without any more trouble.

Chapter 2

Better than a Dumb Ass!

"Serious, Rick!" She underscores the mood change with a loud barefoot slap on the poolside blue stone patio, while shielding her eyes from the sun's glare with her left hand. Two people turned, thinking it may have been a skin-slap. Their frowns quickly became smiles as they saw her smiling while planting her right hand assertively in the channel between thumb and forefinger, on her freshly-tanned but slightly-red, hip.

"We are going to need to play things pretty low key when we return," she says, "or if we return. And assuming we actually plan to stay in Seaport County. Aside from my family, part of me thinks we've probably already had too much to say to too many people there, and should consider moving on. Y'know, like 'get outta Dodge'? I mean, we were on TV, Rick! The whole thing—all that exposure—it makes me nervous."

"Yeah, well," his smiling eyes graze JP's skin, "all that exposure," he says, almost slurring, as he snaps to the awareness that another dozen or so sips from his coconut shell might render him somewhat useless. He sweeps the back of his drink-free hand slowly upwards from her ankles to her shoulders, "all that exposure, and your barefoot patio slap makes me nervous too!"

"Ha-Ha, Rick!" A line of frustration crinkles her brow. "I did say 'serious.' Will you please listen to me? We have to believe that where there's one gangster—as we found out the hard way—there are always more, right?" She puts both hands up now as a visor, almost to emphasize her summary. "We need to be like Thomas Jefferson said, forever on the alert."

"That was Thoreau, Green Eyes. Henry David—Thomas Jefferson urged eternal vigilance. And to be vigilant here, you need a sun visor. Want my baseball cap?"

"Thanks, Professor, but there's not a hill of beans difference. Thoreau and Jefferson were saying the same thing. Besides, Whadda you know? You're just..."—the hint of a grin—"...a business professor! The point is we need to lay low for a while, so to speak. Or, I'm afraid we'll be running the risk of getting into somebody else's gun battle. And I'm not so sure we would be lucky enough to escape another of those scenes—yeah, the, uh, the baseball cap offer? Thanks, but, uh, your head's too big!" She grins.

He nonchalantly pushes his hand through his hair, as if calculating his head size. While leaning to sip from his coconut, he sets his drink concoction on the bar and tests the coconut shell's wobblabilitly before swiveling his stool around to face the low roar of rolling waves. He rests his elbows and bare back against the rounded wood, bar counter edge. He scans the horizon and takes a deep breath.

"Yuppsidoodle, JP! You're right again as usual. I've been so caught up with just being here, I haven't given those kinds of risks much thought. Actually, when you sashayed up to the beer spigots just now, I was recalling the group discussions we led at our last Anchor Out Group Counseling Session aboard the main deck of our live-aboard power boat, the *Here and Now*—now better named the *Then and There*."

He turns partway back to his drink and takes another sip. "It went pretty well, I think—uh, the session that is. I guess we might try doing more of them, y'think?" He nods agreement with himself and continues.

"That little hand-on-hip accompanied foot slap of yours, was, by the way, something of a notable event too! You're kinda cute when you get your temper up and start strutting around, y'know? Hmm? I mean I don't like it when you're mad, but I wouldn't mind a little more of that struttin' stuff." He smiles.

She grins, punches him playfully on the arm, then steps back to toss her wispy hair into the brisk ocean breeze. "You, Professor, are starting to be as big a wise ass as me!"

"Well," he says smiling broadly, "better than a, duh, dumb ass!" They both laugh.

The bartender reaches across the spigots with an umbrella-canopied piña colada "for the young lady—fresh pineapple, fresh coconut, fresh rum" he oozes his word flow while pretending not to notice that her thong disappears into the depths of her buttocks every time she turns sideways.

JP grins, spotlighting her bright white teeth, and highlighting her smile by dimpling up her left cheek, as she reaches for the filled coconut shell. "Thanks, Tico!"

Half leer. Half smile. Tico turns slowly and steps away, periodically checking her out over his shoulder as he moves about behind the bar.

Maddigan's bearded chin pulls back in surprise. He looks puzzled. "You know him?" he asks.

She delays giving him an answer as all four of their eyes follow the server sauntering over to the far end of the bar. Mr. "Tico's" left hand scoops up little piles of cash like a casino dealer while his right-hand plunks down three heavy frosted brown-bottled Belikin beers.

"Imported from Belize," he announces, "over the mountains that stand between us in Nicaragua, Honduras, and Guatemala," Mr. Tico delivers his geography spiel, which he no doubt's found to be worth a little extra tip.

The bartender's just-in-time beer delivery to three middle-aged, heavy-accented German men is overly and graciously acknowledged with exaggerated stage bows, '*danka*'s, and American dollars. The three, by the looks of things, don't seem to care about where the brown bottles came from. They're fully preoccupied with two bikinied twenty-something females six feet to their left, whose hands intermittently sweep hair back over shoulders and pat one another's legs as they jabber about '*home in The Dakotas*.'

Only trouble is, for the Belikin guzzlers, that the young ladies' roaming hands appear more interested in one another than the three men. The Mount Rushmore natives are flaunting their umbrella-canopied piña coladas. One is a few decibels too loud about her "...Boss, the Governor." The other smiles trance-like. She's preoccupied with her drink and smoking—some weird-smelling Made-in-India cigarettes—with her one hand that's not busy inching around her friend's available uncovered skin.

Curiously, JP leans over her own frothy coconut shell, chomping

16

on the dripping slice of decorative pineapple and then sucking deeply on her straw as she watches the action across the bar.

The Germans get rowdier with each new Belikin. Everyone else near the bar has figured out that all five met each other two days earlier in Belize at a Caribbean beach resort at the edge of a rain forest jaguar preserve.

Laughing to herself at the image, JP conjures up of the three drunken Germans in a jaguar preserve, she at last responds to Maddigan's question, "No, you dingbat!" she finally answers. "I don't know the bartender. Costa Ricans call themselves Ticos," she says, "It's in that Frommer's book of yours. The name comes from the tendency that people here have to add a diminutive—either *'tico'* or *'ito'*—to the ends of words in order to," she air-quotes with both arms outstretched, both thumbs holding back her pinkies and ring fingers, while raising and wiggling both of her index and pointer fingers: "in order to connote familiarity or affection." Her hands go to the counter as she continues: "Of course, it makes it a little hard to understand them sometimes. But they really are friendly people, don't you think?"

"Yeah, even more than the little beach honey who just bellied up here and called me a dingbat!" Laughing, Maddigan slides off his stool and stands.

"Beach honey, huh? And what's with the bellied up? I thought you said I sashayed?" She swirls under his arm and slides up against his chest for a kiss: "Mmmmmpf!"

The sun beats down on them as they nuzzle, dreamily, into one another's necks and shoulders, hands softly moving toward each other's hips. They stand close together, enjoying the breezy crosscurrents of salt air and seagull cries that penetrate the roar of the waves.

Like a stun gun, comes a deep voice from two empty bamboo

seats away, "Ah, excuse me? Professor Maddigan?"

Both of them jumped an inch at the same time.

Chapter 3

Farout!

"You are Professor Maddigan, yes?" The voice's source is folded obscurely into the late afternoon glare. Sunlight skims off the ocean's surface. The question chases the frivolity and mounting passion of the moment, and hangs eerily above the bar chatter.

JP steps back. She folds her arms. Her eyelids surrender to a slight twitch between a squint and a glare . . . unsure. she's startled that someone this far away would know Rick's name. Maybe this guy works here, but then how would he know the "Professor" part? That's not on any paperwork the resort would have.

Except for a jagged, well-tanned-over scar that connects his left ear to a bushy moustache that covers his upper lip, the man behind the voice comes into focus. He's a 45-ish, blonde, crooked nose, ex-surfer type. His blue swim trunks emancipated from a Sportlife catalog along with the bright blue and green flowered shirt that's strategically buttoned once above the navel.

A garish gold chain hugs his thick neck and another more delicate one hangs to his sternum. Neither looks like a Cracker Jack prize. Though his arms hint at some serious weight-lifting, he appears harmless enough — yet something about his tone and manner. The intruder slides off his seat and steps toward them

Instantly sober, Rick sits up. "Who wants to know?" he asks defiantly. Sharing what he senses as JP's apprehension, Maddigan slides off his barstool to face the intruder.

"Professor Maddigan? Ms. JP Haley?" (Both their heads snap back ever so slightly!) The intruder nods a bit too ceremoniously to each. The interruption? A minor buzz. Knowing both their names? A major jolt! He steps up close to them and speaks softly,

"My name," he continues, "is Farley Outtinger." He produces and opens an impressive gold shield and credential-card wallet. "Most folks call me 'FarOut,'" he says without batting an eyelash, and not even a hint of amusement. "I'm a private investigator and Special Agent working with the U.S. State Department and U.S. Marshalls under contract with the United States Federal Witness Protection Program."

The Germans are getting rowdy. One drops his Belikin on the patio, snaps his head back and gasps, but the bottle glass is so thick, it bounces. The Belikin group all laughs loudly and one of them orders a replacement for the spillage.

"So, what does all that 'Special Agent' junk have to do with us? And what witnesses are you protecting?" JP shifts her folded arms to a defiant hands-on-hips stance and steps forward... "In other words, Mr. Farout Hotshot: how do you know our names?"

Maddigan nudges her back and speaks under his breath, "JP, please! Chill a minute, will you?"

He then turns back to the Agent to ask questions, but JP interrupts the flow again. This time her teeth are clenched and she snarls briskly back to her partner, "Whaddaya mean, 'chill!'? He knows our names!"

JP is now glaring at the Agent, "Listen up, Mr. Farout, this is

Tuesday. We got here Saturday. You know what that means? It means we're on our third day of our first real vacation, and we're not interested in whatever brought you here, so why don't you just pull up some beach over there," she gestures to the water, "and make like a tourist: swim, fish, get drunk, buy souvenirs. Y'know what I mean? Like just leave us alone!

Go start your own Tourist Protection Program or something. You could probably get federal funding, she says sarcastically. Go for a ten-year study grant—just tell 'em you're helping prevent illegal im-migration. In fact. . . aww forget it!" She turns back to Maddigan and grabs his arm. "C'mon, Rick. Let's take a walk!"

Agent Outtinger nods politely and holds a friendly open hand out urging them to stop. "Ms. JP, please listen for a moment. I can ap-preciate your feelings—your's and the professor's—about having your privacy invaded. I know you both came here seeking stress relief and the chance to recover from your ordeal, and to kind of reinvent your-selves." They both gasp that he knows so much. Outtinger sighs deeply and scans the property.

"That's the part we need to discuss," he continues, "because I'm not the only one here charged with looking for you. Fortunately, I found you first. The others on your trail are invested in preventing you from the pleasurable experience you came here for. They know you're in Costa Rica, but they don't know where. It's just a matter of time 'til they find you—and these people I'm describing are not nice people, Ms. JP."

"How come you know so much about us, and why should we trust you, Farout?" says Maddigan with a touch of sarcasm. "I mean, who the hell are you anyway?" He continues picking up where JP left off, "To barge in here, into our space, out of nowhere, and pretend to protect us from some make-believe threat? Go take a hike!"

As if on cue, JP picks up the pace. "We have nothing to hide, and what makes you think we'll just interrupt our vacation to puppy dog along with you? You, who we don't know from Adam?" Agent Outtinger opens his mouth to respond, but doesn't get a breath out.

"She's right," JP's verbal jab animates the Professor. "I mean what kind of legitimate Special Agent goes prancing around a foreign country resort with a gun under his fancy shirt?"

Outtinger reaches to touch the leather strap through his shirt.

"You really need a better, less obvious shoulder holster, by the way. So, like I was saying—what kind of legit Agent approaches people on vacation trying to wrangle them into some protected witness program?

"And if your I.D.'s a fake, you should know we don't lie down and roll over. In fact, odds are if we don't move faster than you, we'll move a whole lot smarter than you. If you are legit, however, and who you say you are, you're not going to be playing guns and roses in a place and situation like this." JP nods. "So, what gives you the idea we're interested in what you have to say, anyway?"

Again, Outtinger starts to respond, but now it's JP glaring over the tops of her sunglasses, which she lifts to her forehead to accent her squinty stare. She steps on the first word out of the Agent's mouth to take the final verbal punch, speaking to Maddigan but never taking her eyes off the intruder:

"Y'know what, Rick? I agree about Mr. Farout here. Let's just split! We didn't come all this way to relax on vacation just to find another goon like the ones we left behind. Let's go pack and blow this place." She takes Maddigan's arm and steers him two steps away as she waves dismissively at the Agent, "Yeah. See ya, Farout. Happy hunting!"

"Wait! Please! Professor Maddigan, Ms. JP, you need to hear me out. It's my job to make sure you know the risks involved." He talks louder as they keep walking away. "There are quite a few Solamenté Family gangsters who are still on the run."

The couple stops in their tracks at hearing the Solamenté name. They do a quick take at each other, then—eighteen feet away—turn, and slowly walk back to face the now silent "Agent".

"Yes," he says, "Solamenté! You two did a great thing by literally blowing their drug deal out of the water, but the thugs I'm talking about—Gator and Charlton, for example, who never got caught—are still on the run and sworn to find you both at all costs. Their goal is to take you hostage for some obscene amount of ransom money."

"Right!" JP interrupts, "And who exactly do you think will pay to free us? We don't come from any billionaire aristocrat families or something."

"The Seaport County New Jersey government, that's who! Because they want to put an end to Solamenté's control of the whole Jersey Shore—boardwalks, beaches, bars, marinas, restaurants, motels, and government officials— which he runs from his jail cell!

"He has a whole network inside the prison as well as outside. He doesn't care about the money. Ransom money is just a ploy for him to get major media coverage. When he is in all the news headlines, he gets de facto kingship of the federal prison—which he'll put everything on the line for—considering he's going to be there for the rest of his life, and that it's all he can ever have."

Outtinger continues, "But even gaining prison control is just an appetizer. What he's really after is revenge. He's much more interested in seeing each of you die by, by—like, by, some terrible, barbaric, torturous thing—like, uh, staples or something. Y'know what I mean? Like, BIG staples—the kind that roofers use—maybe three quarters of an inch long or something that—applied in certain places—"

JP shivers.

"Well, you can imagine," he says, "that would not be too pleasant. And I'm sure you remember what a sick-o he is, right? I mean he'd enjoy hearing that his goons bled you two to death with three or four thousand big-ass staples. Ya' see what I mean?"

Maddigan grimaces at the thought. JP is stunned. Horrified. She makes a mental note to remember the threat so she could tell her lawyer/book-author girlfriend, Katie Didde, who's always looking for some

23

new angle to build her mystery series around—but she wasn't sure if even Katie would believe the implied intent of Outtinger's disguised outrageous threats. Even that Gator and Charlton mention—those were the two guys who swam away from the Solamenté boat sinking with $12,500,000—not likely they'd be working for Solamenté after robbing him blind, and escaping the law. But that death-by-Staples story conjured up a nauseating mindset.

Visibly shaken by the gruesome example, JP has a sudden flashback vision of how close Solamenté came to ramming a broomstick into her after having his goons tear all her clothes off, forcibly spread her legs apart and then hold them apart, while he toyed with threatening to ram the filthy splintering broomstick.... JP is visibly repulsed at even recalling those horrible few moments —a disgusting thought, even in a fiction context—not to mention the reality of her anger and fear.

Maddigan, recalling that horror, with his hands tied behind his back and one closed black-eye he was dealt while trying to save JP, is equally repulsed at the evil, crass reminder of being forced to watch as she held her breath. Those agonizing clock-ticks seemed like eternity before Solamenté finally stepped away at the last minute, and ordered his goons to let them both go. Maddigan, wrists finally untied, settled her with a quiet hand against the small of her back. His other hand then a fist. And this minute—here and now—Maddigan's other hand is once again a fist. Recalling all of that right now, both of them get goosebumps. JP quivers.

Chapter 4

Ach du Lieber!

"We're talkin' 'bout a man who's a mental case here," Agent Out-tinger continues. "He'd like nothin' more than to laugh at hearing how you both lose your eyes and tongues and private parts to torturous, timed, industrial staple-gun blasts . . . like one every minute or two for hours on end..."

Outtinger pauses to let that thought settle in. He smirks at their quivering, then quickly scans the poolside bar and patio to make sure no one's moved within earshot.

"So," he continues, "we hear Solamenté has had second thoughts now in prison. He wants both of you to suffer slow deaths—as he puts it—for killing his son, and for busting up his drug deal. He wants you both dead, but he wants it on his terms so he's got all kinds of low-life gangsters out looking for you and for the two bad-guy fishermen who worked for him—Gator and Charlton. They got away with the $12.5 million that was never recovered from his $25 million total.

"He got word that those two dudes are holed up somewhere in

a Caribbean jungle between Belize and Panama which includes Honduras, Nicaragua, and here: Costa Rica. And that's why I'm carrying a gun. Now, are you two starting to put this together? Solamenté wants national headlines. He sees himself as the second coming of Al Capone. And he sees the two of you as the missing link he needs to eliminate in order to make that happen. You get what I'm saying?"

"Sure thing, FarOut," Maddigan blurts out, "but we can't live our lives hiding from that piece of dirt."

"The Professor is right," JP says, still quivering, "thanks for the heads up! We'll be on the alert. Now you can consider your job done and be on your merry way back to Washington. Oh, and when you get there, tell the President we said 'Hey!' And tell your boss, by the way, that the bottom line for us is that neither one of us is interested in getting any help from anybody. We are not collecting food stamps or unemployment or looking for ANY kind of public assistance. We can take care of ourselves and," she pauses to remember Outtinger's warning, "if there's no other choice, Mr. FarOut: most offices —even including the front desk at this place— have staple removers, so . . ."

Outtinger, now patting the part of his shirt that covers his holster, interrupts her: "Let me put it this way, Ms. JP:" He steps toward them, looks left then right and lowers his voice: "The government wants to take out the whole Solamenté Mob Family, and I didn't come here to ask you to cooperate. I'm here to tell you that you must cooperate. There are three other Agents here with me now..." He pauses to let that info sink in, then adds: "And we are in view of all three right now, as we speak."

JP's and the Professor's darting eyes do a quick scan around the perimeter of the grounds. There are scores of people —alone and in clusters— scattered about. Some seem to be casually glancing their way.

"It's their job, and mine, to make sure that you are both returned to the United States pronto, and that you will change your IDs. The four of us here, who will escort you, adds up to one agent for each of your arms —plus an award-winning federal pitbull, named P-Bite." He glares at Maddigan. "P-Bite is nearby and waiting for my whistle."

Maddigan scans again and wonders why the dog's not to be seen. "So," Outtinger continues, "bottom line is: like it or not, you're both leaving here with me, It's not a matter of choice. It's a requirement." The two of them are stunned by that message.

He pats his shirt again as he lets his directive sink in. "I expect, and am truly hopeful... that you won't make this any more difficult than it already is, that you'll cooperate with what I'm telling you if you want to prevent me and my four assistants from us from having to use force to bring you back (and, of course, spare yourselves from me signaling P-Bite)."

He takes a deep breath. The P, by the way, stands for (he looks both ways again then stares at Maddigan's swimming trunks): Pecker." Maddigan grimaces. JP squints.

He stops talking abruptly as the Belikin Beer bottle bouncer barges briskly —and drunk— into and between the three of them, laughing and stumbling. "Ach du lieber!" he yells. Their eyes all follow as the man heads for a beach belly-flop into a receding wave, nearly missing the water altogether. Maddigan's grimace turns to a comical wince. JP pokes him in the ribs. Both return their attention to the reality of the stern-faced self-proclaimed "Agent."

Outtinger is scoping out the German man's laughing friends who are still yucking it up across the bar. Seemingly satisfied that none of the others in that group were rushing out to follow their drunken friend, he turns back to his threatening tone, and to outline his prescribed departure plan.

"We have a special plane waiting with pre-paid first-class seats for you. You have," he checks his watch, "twenty minutes to get back to your cottage and pack!"

Outtinger takes a deep breath before wrapping up. "The other three Agents and I (and P-Bite) will be making sure you comply. We'll get you to the plane. Your resort bill —including these drinks here and staff tips— are already paid. You will have first-class room and meal accommodations when we land, as well as all during the coming weeks, while you are receiving orientation training regarding your new identities.

"And ALL public exposure," he continues, "and ALL contact with friends and families will be avoided during this time, beginning right now. Your cottage phone was disconnected." He pauses, then adds, "You will come to see that all this is for your own good. Spare us from having to handcuff and drag you!" He checks his watch again. "Twenty minutes!"

Their eyebrows raised and mouths agape, Maddigan and JP stand motionless, absorbing the words. Outtinger continues: "These people who are looking for you will think nothing of stripping your skin off with razor-sharp potato peelers, hacking off your fingers, hands, feet and... your heads...then dumping your parts into some super-sealed luggage that they privately fly to New Jersey's biggest airport where airport officials are paid handsomely to keep their mouths shut and deliver your parts to The Mob's Concrete Foundation Team in the bowels of downtown riff-raff." He pauses and half-grins. "Y'get what I mean?"

He looks around before delivering the final thought: "So," he summarizes, "ignore what I'm telling you and you become permanent, never-to-be-found ingredients in the foundation of some new mob-owned football stadium or lowlife highrise, y'know what I mean?"

JP swallows hard at this new thought, which actually trumped the staples image in her mind. Maddigan is repulsed by both the imagery and the source. He sees JP flinch.

"At least this way," Outtinger continues, "you get a second chance on life until we can nail these guys. And P-Bite gets some real dog food to chomp on instead of your butts, or—" he smiles at the thought, "— Other more important parts!"

"So, I'm sorry to interrupt your vacation, folks, but at least when you're done with me, you'll still be able to walk and . . ." He stops to look around, then lifts his left eyebrow as if to gain a better look at the descent of JP's thong. "And, uh, party," he says a bit too snarly.

"So," he wraps up with one final pat on the bump under his shirt, "we need to get a move on. Now! Go dress and pack up your things quickly. We meet here in twenty minutes, okay?" They both nod and walk briskly toward their cottage.

They hustle along the path toward the main resort building and activity center, past other cottages, toward the one they've just settled into at the end of the waterfront path, JP whispers quickly, "Rick, we can't do this. I mean how the hell do we know if this guy is for real? It's hard to believe he would talk this way with us if he was."

She glances over her shoulder and takes a breath, but before he can respond, she continues: "Y'know, anybody can carry a badge around. And where are those mysterious three other Agents? They sure as shit aren't those German clowns or their two flirty bimbette targets. And where's the dog he's threatening with? This could be a set-up for all we know. Maybe Farout even works for Solamenté," she whispers.

"I know, JP, I know. I agree. He's a bit too loosey-goosey to be convincing. And I just don't like the lengths he goes to with his torture descriptions. it's a little too much like he's the one charged with carrying out the orders, or else he has an awfully perverted imagination or has spent a few years in jail himself listening to the horror stories of those who were locked in there with him. We don't have the time and we can't take the chance to find out. The bottom line is that we have to think and act pretty damn fast here and now, and I don't have any answers." They continue to hustle along the path. "On the other hand," Maddigan continues, "what is it they say about erring on the side of caution?"

Their eyes continue to dart back and forth between each other's faces.

"Yeah," says JP. After a few more steps, she nods and points her chin sideways for Maddigan to follow the gesture as they near the last hundred feet of walkway. They look at each other. She whispers, "And so, what exactly is it that they say, Professor, that opportunity only comes to those who look for it!?"

He follows her nod and glances sideways between cottage units, through the open breezeway, and instantly understands her meaning. He nods, and says, "Gotcha!" At that same moment, they reach their door and rush madly inside. Talk is not necessary. They both know exactly what they need to do.

They lock the door, grab their wallets and passports, the in-room stationery set, binoculars, and the 3-D, 5½ x 6, framed woodcut of a stucco jungle house that a local artist sold them on the beach after breakfast, plus two quarts of local rum they purchased at the resort guest shop. They pick up their hiking boots, Maddigan's folding four-inch blade Buck knife, plus an armful of clothes and a beach towel each. They hold out the towels and jam all the rest quickly into their nylon backpacks which they snatch up as they head for the back door.

"C'mon, JP. We'll change later. We can get new toothbrushes someplace. Right now, we've got ten minutes left to go POOF! and disappear!" On their way out the back slider-door facing the beach, they each grab one of the gaucho hats that were waiting for them in their room when they arrived.

"Nine!" she says. He responds: "What? 'Nein?' – No? What do you mean, NO?"

"You've been listening to those knockwurst guys at the bar too much. I wasn't talking German, you goofball! We have nine minutes," she whispers loudly, glancing at the clock, "not ten!"

Chapter 5

Rum n' Coax!.

Still in bathing suits, but now with beach towels over their shoulders they cautiously open the back slider-door then tip-toe through the porch railing gate, and quietly click it closed. They look both directions and amble casually down the beach hugging their backpacks to their chests, between themselves and the water, and out of view from anyone and everyone who are all behind them.

With low-keyed stealth, they step casually up onto the resort dock, where they climb aboard the single motor launch—tied to the pier with the engine still running—they'd spotted between the rows of cottages.

Logan, the boat boy, as he'd probably been doing for years, left it tied with one rope loop while headed to the main building kitchen for a quick take-out container of coffee or rum.

Maddigan keeps his eyes fixed on the beach bar area as he slides into the control seat. He sees Mr. Farout chatting up some topless country bumpkin blonde who has spilled into a poolside lounge chair.

"Thank God again for sex." He laughs.

They toss backpacks to the center floorboards as JP connects something to the rope that's affixed to the dock's tie-up post before pulling the boat's tie-up rope casually away and tossing it to Maddigan; she then drops quickly to the boat's floor, out of sight between their backpacks. Maddigan tugs on the chinstrap of his wide-brimmed hat to cover most of his face, hunkers down into towel resting over his shoulders. Then he hunches down over the controls, tucks the tie-up rope under his seat and chugs the boat away at walking speed.

A hundred yards out, he kicks up the engine. Just as he does, they hear a distant "Hey!" from Logan who is waving from the dock but appears to be laughing. Maddigan can't figure that one out, but sees that nobody near the bar seems to notice him and JP, as they speed around the harbor corner marked by a fifty-foot-high wall of boulders, immediately hiding them.

Out of view from the resort, JP sits up. Both of them loosen their chinstraps and drop the towels from their shoulders to their feet. Maddigan opens engine power and levels the launch off to a plane as they ride atop the slow rolling tide change from high to low, or maybe ebb. They head for open waters north along the jungle coast, toward Nicaragua, with no idea where they are or where they're going, but the boat's gas tank is full and it's a beautiful ride on a beautiful day—the third day of their reward-money vacation.

They laugh at the tangle they imagine having left behind—Agent FarOut and his mysterious three other agents scrambling around, checking rooms, making urgent calls, harassing staff.

"Y'know," Maddigan says, "I can't help but think about that poor dog, P-Bite, having to eat dog food." He grins at the thought, but then turns serious. "Anyway, I do feel bad about taking the kid's boat. He's probably gonna get hell from his boss. I hope he's not fired for it!"

"Gonna get hell, Professor? Gonna?" mocks JP, who begins a long slow wide grin. "What the hell is *gonna*? Who talks like that? A professor talks like that? Jeeze! Anyway," she says, smiling, "you don't gotta worry cause when Logan got to the dock, he found one of our white cottage stationery envelopes with a big, letters TO LOGAN on it taped to his red, foul weather, gear jacket looped onto the piling hook where he had tied the launch rope. And, guess what? Inside, he found a Traveler's Check payable to the resort—enough to buy a brand-new launch—plus a bunch of cash to get himself a couple of extra rum drinks in exchange for what we gonna need him to do, which is to locate Mr. Farout and tell him he saw us headed inland into the rain forest."

She laughs at the astonished look on Maddigan's face, as he whispers to himself, but just loud enough for her to hear him: "THAT'S why he was laughing when he yelled!"

"Hey, Rick, that's why I'm on this team. I mean one of us has to be able to think while the other packs a backpack and then captains' the motor launch—I hope you got my boots!"

"Uh, your boots, eh?" He feigns a snarl. "Well, I got your left one there, Green Eyes. Was I supposed to bring both?" They laugh and hug. The launch splashes fearlessly along, half a mile offshore. The idea of finding a place to buy toothbrushes fades rapidly as they take turns following the jungle beach coastline through the binoculars, hopeful of spotting a safe, secure-looking haven where they can spend the night, ditch the boat and move on.

So far, there's nothing in view except dense jungle backed by dense mountains, and dense cloud puffs in an endless blue sky, above the glittering Pacific.

Two hours pass quickly. Dry patches of getting redder skin prompt them to put shorts and tees over their bathing suits. The constant salt water spray camouflages the sunburn reality. Deciding to stay barefoot for the time being, they pull their heavy socks from the backpack and tuck them into their hiking boots. JP uses the laces to lash the four boots to the shuddering gunnel racks that hold the life preservers.

The boots thump between waves. She pads them with the towels.

The spectacular, never ending view continues to mesmerize them. There are no other boats in sight, and they see nothing but the vast sea, empty of watercraft on one side and close to the waters edge jungle with a backdrop of alternately rocky then forested mountains on the other.

The motor hums. The water slaps. A long wake behind them that splits the waves into equal trails is followed by a cluster of low-gliding gulls diving into the water behind them as the boat wake churns silvery seagull lunchtime flashes of tiny fish up to the surface. It seems like another hour has gone by.

"Y'know, JP, from best I can figure, we're still in Costa Rica, headed north—I believe toward Nicaragua, and El Salvador, which I've heard are not real friendly places. We need to get past those two countries to get to Guatemala which gives us a straight shot over the Guatemalan mountains and jungle. From there we can get to the Caribbean and connect with someplace like Belize, then decide from there.

"My author-friend Mike Slosberg," he continued, "told me about a trip he took to Belize and mentioned the Hmmmmmm Hummingbird Highway as the way to the Caribbean as long as—according to Mike—you hum!" She grinned.

He continued, "the hard part's figuring out how we can get all the way across to the Caribbean without getting discovered. Once we do, I know places we can go in Bonaire and the Dominican Republic. Anyway, since you've always liked adventure—"

Something in his statement seems to her to have the makings of a quip, but the view and sense of freedom shift her mental gears. She holds her tongue instead, as she takes in the vastness of jungle and mountains to the right, and endless horizon to the left.

"Thanks, Mike Slosberg," she whispers, then hums to herself, unheard above the motor and waves thumping port side.

Minutes pass. She speaks up above the engine noise, "Well, we're headed somewhere, yes? How will we ever know when we get there?

Is there like a Washington Bridge between the two countries, like between New York and New Jersey? Or WELCOME signs, or a border patrol or something like between Texas and Mexico? Or a buncha marker buoys? Or do we just slowly fold from one country into the other? And when? How far is —"

Maddigan laughs, "No!" He laughs again. "No, there's NO like Washington Bridge or buncha buoys. Man, you sure do ask a lot of questions. Is that how you got good grades in my classes?"

"HA! I got good grades from you, Professor, because I am good! And, my name, in case you didn't notice me in my new bikini, is not 'Man', man!"

"C'mon now, JP, who could not notice? The bartender's teeth nearly fell out every time you turned your sweet little buns his way, and I—"

He stops mid-sentence. They both seem to spot the cove at the exact same time. Maddigan grabs the binoculars.

"We should mosey on in closer to see what looks like a breathing space in the coastline. No people or boats I can see, but how about we check it out?" She nods.

Maddigan turns the motor launch toward the cove, which looks to be about three-quarters of a mile away. The strip of beach sand looks about fifty yards wide, surrounded by heavy jungle with glimpses of high-rise cliffs patched in between. No signs of life, which could be good—or bad.

They chug slowly toward the border of the palms, white sand oasis, wrapped in bird calls, and sparkling white-capped, rolling waves. The boat scrapes bottom as they shut off the motor, raise the prop out of the sand and hop out into knee-deep water to pull the launch through the ebbs and exert themselves to drag it up onto the beach. They stand, look, and listen.

After hours of motor hum, and waves lapping and slapping the bow and transom, splashing over the gunnels, the newfound silence seems deafening.

Maddigan unscrews the clamps that hold the almost 100 pound motor so he can take it off. He staggers up the beach with it to rest it against a large tree trunk.

Using rounded pieces of driftwood intermittently placed as rollers under the bottom of the boat, the two of them tug the launch through the sand, stop, move the rollers up the beach in front of the bow, and keep repeating that for a hundred feet of sand, past the high-water mark of seaweed, broken shells, palm leaves, strips of bark and spindly bits of branches.

Scurrying bursts of foam splay across the sand with each wave. They both sit, catch their breath, and lean against the launch. They watch and listen to the quiet as if some part of each of them knows they are in the eye of the dreaded unspoken calm before the storm they may yet need to face. Both knew that Solamenté, not the weather, was the issue.

Suddenly they hear it. Like something out of an old Western TV movie—though some might think the faintly audible distant drums unnerving—they smile instead and shrug at the idea.

"I don't think Mafia guys play drums in jungles," she said with a big grin.

He smiled back. "Y'know what, Green Eyes? I agree. And I know we're both woofed, but it is getting late and gonna be dark before we know it. We should probably drag the boat to hide behind some of those fallen palm trees, turn it over, and plan to sleep under it for the night, then get a fresh start in the morning.

"There's still a good amount of gas left," he continues, "so we'll have some choices to make when the sun comes up. But—for now— happy vacation, Baby! I'm glad to be here with you."

"Well, Rick, I'm sure you know it, but I'll say it anyway. I'm glad to be with you too! Y'think a quick skinny-dip to jet down before our rum and cheese chunks between the crusty French bread dinner might be in order? I did manage to grab half a loaf of bread and two slabs of breakfast cheese on our way out the door. And, uh, you got the rum, yes?"

"Seriously? Do you think of everything, JP? And yes, I do indeed, have the rum!"

"Good, cause food and rum are pretty important when running from government agents who want to kidnap us, change our identities, hold us for ransom, cut off our fingers and that makes me want to give 'em the finger, y'know?"

He grins a huge grin: "What would I ever do if I didn't have you to make me laugh?"

"I don't know, but you'd better figure out that sleeping thing you said, y'know? The under the upside-down boat stuff? Like how do we do that with just one blanket, two wet towels and windbreakers, and especially when we both wanna jump each other's bones?"

They laugh. "Hmmm, well a couple of wet towels underneath will keep us cool and one blanket and the bone-jumping part works just fine if one of us is on top," he says.

She responds, "Well, I think you're pretty cool and it doesn't much matter to me who's on top, so I'll drink to that! Only trouble is I haven't seen a Coke machine, and it doesn't look like we're likely to find any ice here, but, where's the rum?"

"How about a skinny-dip first?" Maddigan strips and stumbles to the water. JP follows, peeling off her clothes. They splash, laugh, cling, kiss and hug their way back to the bread, cheese, blanket, and bottle of rum, under the upside-down boat.

Chapter 6

Locks 'n Bagels

Apple Solamenté's brain feels upside-down. No sleep. He paces his Southern California, windowless, six-foot square solitary confine-ment prison cell all day and into the night. He keeps a distance from everyone but his three closest confidants during their afternoon 'Fresh Air Break,' where the four of them meet daily when it's not raining or 100-plus degrees in the heavily-guarded, forty-foot high-walled, ra-zor-wire ringed courtyard.

It had taken him months to recover from the professor's errant gunshot wound, and then find out in his restored consciousness that his only son Benjamin had died in the same brutal gunfire. Of course, the wounded mob leader conveniently forgot that it was he who mur-dered someone, and that it was he who ignited the entire gunfight and tortured the professor and his girlfriend in the first place—the same he who put his own son in a dirt grave forever.

Ignoring this revelation was, to Solamenté, almost as important as his need to have a coordinated appearance—even in prison. He wears a specially-ordered, elasticized, gray washcloth material headband, and matching socks. All of this to fit with Apple's Brillo-pad hair that he's growing back after being cuffed to the barber chair and throwing up at the horrific experience of getting a new prisoner razor-cut head shave.

Beyond matching his gray head and feet, the thirty-minute court-yard breaks are his only escape. He's allowed no visitors. And reality is that these blips of fresh air may well be his only sense of freedom for forever. Stepping out into the weather three or four days a week gives him chance to walk, scheme, plot, and figure out how to get even. He and his gangster sidekicks share the hopelessness of clinging to and out living the system.

In hushed, gravely-animated mutterings, Solamenté rails nonstop about what has to be done, when, and by whom. His every statement triggers quiet nods of agreement from cell block mates Bo, Chop, and Phil, who listen intently as their combined five eyes scan the yard activity and assess every movement of the caffeined-up, muscle-beach, pistol-packing, speed-freak guards strolling the tower walls.

The whispers begin: "Maddigan and that tight-ass bitch of his have to die. That's it! There's no other way. Nothin' else can possibly avenge them for wastin' my son." Apple sniffles, snorts, and blows his nose between his thumb and forefinger, flinging the end result slimy contents into a feeble-looking patch of weeds between the two stone benches that the four of them occupy—where it clings to, and oozes off, an errant dandelion.

"We gotta torture 'em both to their last breath. And, y'know what, Chop Sooey? If you was outside, you'd be my man to cut 'em into pieces—but at least we got Outtinger. He can do the job—him and that flaky broad who works for some Podunk governor—plus those two drunken creeps he pals around with. They're all a little short on the uptake, if y'know what I mean? Thing is, they all got big balls—yeah, even the broad! Hahaha!"

Apple pulls a lumpy napkin from under his shirt and unwraps a smuggled buttered bagel. He stuffs a third of it into the opening under his bushy gray mustache and makes a token offer to the three members of his listening audience. They shake their heads side-to-side ever so slightly. None reach for a bite. Chop's one eye remains fixed on Apple's disgusting yellow-green phlegm dripping slow-motion off the weeds. Apple's mouth still full, he takes another chomp.

Phil Thee follows Apple's whispers with his own as he pats the Boss gently on the back in a show of agreement.

"If anybody can pull it off, Boss, it's Outtinger, and he's got one eye more than Chop, here." Phil Thee looks at Sooey. "Hey, Chop, no offense. You cut off fingers better than most guys with two eyes. It's just that Outtinger's a sneaky bastard and will know how to lure those two into his own workspace, y'know what I mean?" Sooey nods agreement.

"Yeah," Bo's guarded, husky half-voice quietly chimes in. "Outtinger's okay so long as he don't get himself tangled up with some broad. Yeah, He's a damn sucker for exhibitionist bimbos—the kind that hang out at them resort beaches."

Still whispering, "Hey!" Bagel particles fly out of Solamenté's mouth as he swallows a quiet string of coughs, "Maybe I need to arrange to get him fixed like that whacko pit bull he drags around with him when he's working downtown, y'know?" Another muffled cough. "Whazzhiz name, Bo? That mutt? P-B or sumtin'?

"Yup! Calls him Peckerbite, Boss. Claims he's taken out a buncha dicks with those fangs of his."

Chop and Phil Thee pull back their heads, exchange squeamish squint while subconsciously moving their hands to cover their crotches, then babble off a stream of pretend chuckles. Solamenté's bagel-filled mouth emits a muffled laugh along with a small chunk of poppy-seeded butter. He coughs. He drools.

The four of them sneak sweeping glances around the yard to see if their whispering jabber is attracting attention. It's not. Head down, Apple attacks his bagel more tenaciously, dissolving his three-second-long fake grin as he chews, then clears his throat to resume his whisper —and the whole conversation ends up being whispered.

"Listen up Mr. Bo Strangles! If Outtinger screws up, I want you to put the word out to finish him off. The man knows too much to fail us on this mission. Get your guys to starve his mutt into a frenzy, then lock 'em both in the closet."

Strangles grins at the idea. "And—" Solamenté cuts his whispered words pointedly between muffled coughs—"if that's what we decide to do, you make sure that everyone in here, guards included, knows that the order came from my cell! Got that? We'll make an example of his ass."

Apple checks the clouds, something he never did before prison fresh-air breaks.

"Of course, if the man delivers," he adds, "he should live to see another day, in which case, maybe a little groin injury will calm him down. I once had a barking little yip-yap that was making me crazy, but he turned into a pansy after he got fixed. HA! Outtinger might even have to change his name from FarOut to Embedded HA! HA! HA!"

"You got it, Boss," says Bo, covering his mouth with his hairy gnarled fingers, "I'd strangle him and his crotch-chompin' dog both— all by myself if I could get outta here. But since it don't look like I'm walkin' anytime soon, I'll be happy to make a call to order the man's de-dicktification. Just say the word and Peckerbite goes on a starvation diet!"

They all stare into space and immediately stop whispering as one of the guards passes. Solamenté rocks slowly on the concrete bench. Once out of the guard's earshot, he starts whispering again. "Good," he huffs to Strangles. Then addresses all three.

"What we need to do now is nail those two slime balls that took off with my twelve and a half mil." Heads nod. "Seems odd to me that they're supposta be in the same area as the professor and his bitch. A little too coincidental, y'think? Bo?"

41

Strangles sneers, tightens his fists. Apple adjusts his headband, turns to Phil Thee, and asks, "Anything new?"

"Not yet, Boss, but FarOut says he has a clue."

"Is that right?" Solamenté asks, as he stuffs the rest of his bagel down. "So, maybe we just skip the pit bull thing and just tie Outtinger down for some roto-rooter neutering with a rusted reciprocating saw until he comes up with some answers about his clue—y'know what I mean, Sooey?"

Chop responds with a sneer. He, as Apple knows, is particularly fond of the demolition damage a reciprocating saw can do, which is what got him life in prison to start with. Solamenté shifts his weight and grins, then continues,

"Unless he spills the beans right away, maybe we just take one testicle and give him another mission, huh?"

He coughs then whispers, "I want them twelve-and-a-half big bucks back as much as I want those two hoo-ha's chopped in little pieces and ground into concrete."

The deafening horn-blasts reverberate throughout the courtyard. Fresh Air Time is over. Guards appear. Whistles blow. All eighty-plus inmates fall into line and begin slogging their way back to their cells. Apple's at the core in the middle of the pack. His eyes dart and land on one of the guards he's approaching. He drops the bagel wrapper discreetly between the 159 shuffling feet—and Phil Thee's wooden leg. The nearest guard picks up the crumpled napkin, sees Solamenté's writing and stuffs it into his pocket.

Chapter 7

Pot Luck!

The distant drums that ushered in their sleep are still. All's silent now but for the waves and passing gull cries. Shards of light poke between mountain treetops. Maddigan rubs his eyes.

"Hey, Green Eyes, time for us to get up and get a move on. We're lookin' at a long day ahead, and need to make the most of travel time."

"Yeah, well good morning to you too, Professor!" Still on her back, she rolls toward him. They both crawl out from under the upside-down wooden boat and dress quickly, brushing sand away as they wince, easing their sunburned feet into hiking socks and boots.

JP grabs the backpacks and pulls them to the side. "So," she then gestures to the launch and motor, "what do we do with these?"

"Well, since we paid for both, I guess we own 'em, right? How about we pour the motor gas over the boat—uh, very carefully—then rub two Girl Scouts together to make a fire and then we walk away, hmmm?"

"Rubbing Girl Scouts? Honestly, Rick, you are totally couthless!"

"Nah, I still have some teeth!"

"Couthless, you wacko, not Toothless!"

"Wacko, eh? Well sink your teeth into this. we need to make like in hockey and get the puck outta here!" She responds to his hockey puck reference with a snarl.

"And since you've thought of everything else, Ms. Green Eyes, I imagine you brought a Zippo lighter along for the occasion?"

She pulls half a dozen wooden matches out of her pocket from the room stationery packet she salvaged.

Grateful for her saving the day yet again, Maddigan deep-sixes the clown act, and mutters, "You ARE amazing, woman!" as he twists off the gas cap.

The two of them hoist the motor high enough to carefully pour the remaining gallon or so of gas across the bottom-up keel. They hide the motor in the dense surrounding shrubbery.

She strikes the match on a rock, cups it in her hands, tosses the flame at the rivulet of gas running down the transom, and the boat ignites instantly. The sudden flash and burst of heat force them both to step back quickly, fifteen or twenty feet, toward the water's edge.

They sling their packs over their shoulders, then stand and watch for a moment.

Assured nothing visible will remain, except the metal oarlocks and motor corpse, they look around, then head for what looks remotely like a sand path through the jungle.

Distancing themselves from the glowing flames, they trudge off through the soft sand as dawn unfolds into daylight. Turning occasionally to look back, they eventually lose sight of the dying flames and smoke that the tide change has enabled. And they begin to connect more with the trail and their changing surroundings.

The sandy path transitions from beach to moisture-ridden undergrowth with rock outcroppings, accompanied by continuous and unusual scattered bird calls.

They step over fronds, termite mounds and parades of fire ants—

that by the thousands, are carrying their salvaged bird-and-fish-parts-prey to family banquets. For nearly two hours, the couple tromps through mud and underbrush, following a gradually increasing loud roar. They arrive, finally, at the source: a small clearing marked by a large waterfall, and bursting sunshine.

"Wow, Rick! Pretty neat place, huh?"

"You got that right, JP. Maybe the prettiest thing I've ever seen." He glances her way and sees a pout surfacing. "Ah, except of course for you, M'lady!" From the outer corners of both pairs of eyes, the two of them exchange squinty little smile lines.

As they continue their path in silence, at a slower, more determined pace, a sudden nearby rustling of shrubs triggers them to turn quickly, and a bit fearfully—just in time to see a gorgeous rainbow-colored parrot squawking noisily as it flutters up and away.

"Whew!" he says, "It's not often something so beautiful as a parrot prompts such a rush of blood to the head."

Relieved, they laugh nervously, turn back to face one another, then continue hiking.

"Oh, Professor, you always have the right words. But, pre-parrot you know, you called me your *lady* and truth is, I'm not really much of a lady," as she follows him over a couple of large boulders.

"This is true," he says. "You're definitely not a lady—don't know whatever possessed me—but you and your green eyes're way more beautiful than that parrot! And, besides, even though you ain't hardly no lady, I love you anyway."

She fawns. They both laugh. They drop their backpacks and pull up seats on the nearest boulder to watch the falls.

"Strange bird calls," she comments loudly to compensate for the cascading roar that muffles their voices.

"Yeah, nothing like Jersey Shore seagulls," he shouts back. They laugh. She snuggles against his shoulder. They know they need to get moving, yet they daydream.

"Yo!"

They jump! A man's voice rises above the din. A touch of unfamiliar accent. They both snap alert, hoping it's not another federal agent type. But as they turn, they're relieved to see a tall, thin, bare-chested black man with a bandanna tied around his head. Dreadlocks, and a leather bag slung over one shoulder. Maddigan stands.

"So firsd, you discover my falls, and flush out my beaudiful parrod bird" the stranger accuses them loudly with a smile, "and nexd you will come to our drums. And if da snakes don ged you, Mon, da lizards will make you creepy-crawly."

The man drops his bag next to theirs and sits facing them with his back to the falls.

JP surveys him over the tops of her sunglasses. Maddigan scans the area where the man emerged and, satisfied that their guest is alone, sits back down. Both men reach to shake hands at the same time.

"Me be Rico!" the stranger announces, "Rico, with an "O" as in flow, dough and glow. But I am a famous Jamaican, Mon, from Pord Andonio, only sixdy miles from Kingsdon, bud aboud coupla days drivin' 'round podholes, Mon," he says, laughing. "Oh! And I can'd say dadd number dwendy ledder in da alphabed—someding aboud da nerves in my doung—oh ya gadda be payshon wid me do unders dand my dalk—das okay wid you?"

"Well, of course, Rico. In fact, your version of the alphabet sounds more friendly anyway. And me be Rick!" Maddigan announces back in friendly mimicry, "as in brick, sick, slick, click, flick, lick and trick—but nothing famous like you—and I am from the Jersey Shore, eight million people and eight million potholes away from New York City," continues Maddigan, before finishing off with a hearty laugh.

"Ah, Americano, Si? Perhaps Rickshaw would work for explaining your name, bud den dad is for Chinese, yes? You are from Daxicab Life in the Big Apple ciddy area, and only ead Chinese wid chopsix, yes?" They all laugh. "And you?" He stands to shake hands with JP.

"And I'm JP," she says. "My name is sorta like, Uh, JD as in Juvenile Delinquent or JKLMNOP as in alphabet soup, or sounds like JV ."

"Junior Varsidy, Mon. I god id!" All three laugh again.

"Yeah, but I have no icky pothole problems," she adds. And yet another laugh.

"So, what you dune here, Mon, on the edge of Guanacasde Peninsula? I mean dis is like nowhere, y'know? Y'lossed? Or jus cruisin'—or waidin' for me?

"Well," Maddigan says, stretching his legs, "that all depends on why we might be, uh—waiting for you."

"Could be I have some—how you say?—knock-your-socks-off ganja," the Jamaican says with a twinkle in his eye.

"Whoa there! Sounds great, Mr. Rico-as-in-Puerto, but we've a long hike ahead of us, and we'll never get past the waterfalls here if we start smoking pot at this time of day. Besides," Maddigan adds, if you knock my socks off, I'll get blisters on my feet!"

"He's right, Rico," JP chimes in quickly, "but we have some rum if you'd like?"

"Hahaha, Mz. JKLMNOP. No dank you. Rum is in my blood. Id maybe even insdead of my blood. Here, rum is like, like you drink wadder." He pauses and looks around. "Bud I could use some Ganga. Mind if I lighd up?"

"Hey, help yourself. Get stoned on the rocks," she laughs. "Ha, ha! Anyway, it's been nice meeting you, but we need to get moving—"

"I dell you whad you doo needs," Rico interrupts, "My bessed guess is dad you don' maybe need any pod, bud you need maybe some podluck —like maybe I guide you to a village where you can figure out how to ged where you're going. He stands and smiles. "C'mon," he says. "Follow me."

JP and Maddigan exchange eye contact, shoulder shrugs, and smiles. Minutes later, they are leaving the falls together, the Jamaican in the lead, puffing on his joint, headed further up into the mountains —

the silence in such contrast to the roar they left behind—every leaf-rustle, every twig-snap a major event.

"Oh," says Rico, like he was leading a group of city-dwellers on a National Geographic photography expedition, "Ya mighd wanna make a lodda noise wid yer feed every once in a while, my friends, do keep da snakes dad live up here away from dah padway. Lodsa raddlesnakes here. Somedimes dey hang from da drees also so don' sid down undil you firsd look up! Yah?" Rico takes a deep breath then adds, "Probably nod much differend dan whad I hear is like dealing wid da Mafia in New Jersey, Mon, yes?

Maddigan appeared a bit startled at first by the Mafia reference, but then smiled. JP's mind wanders back to her girlfriend Katie Didde, who she's certain would fall in love instantly with Rico and his love for "D"s instead of "T"s. JP grins.

Some of Rico's joint-puffs kept finding their way over his shoulders past JP, who gave it a couple of quiet sniffs en route to Maddigan's nose, but the Professor—she was pleased to see—seemed more preoccupied with wondering about where Rico was leading them.

Chapter 8

Rico Puffs Away!

Hours of rock, dirt, hanging vines, ant parades and termite mounds. Crackly brown palm fronds, and rainbows of parrots replace the sounds of now-more-distant gulls, but thankfully, no rattlesnakes!

They move onward through refreshingly cool mountain breezes. Always the bare brown heels of Mr. Rico—as in Puerto—seem to glide and guide them between patches of sunshine.

At the beckoning of shifting air currents, cotton puffs of clouds drift past them high above, while periodic whiffs of marijuana float up their noses. Maddigan's past pot addiction temptations have slowly continued to rise to the surface with periodic third-in-line inhalations and exaggerated sniffs. JP senses his struggle to keep his mouth shut, and nudges him with occasional elbow bumps and smiles.

They trek further inland, stealing glimpses here and there of the increasingly jungle-obscured and more distant Pacific Ocean.

In the time JP thought it would have taken to hike the Jersey Shore miles through oceanfront sand between Point Pleasant and Seaside Heights' boardwalks—had they been blanketed with hills—and have second thoughts about whether they should or shouldn't have agreed to follow this guy, they come to a clearing that overlooks a tiny, picturesque fishing village tucked into a remote cove a few hundred feet below.

The three of them slowly and carefully descend the rocky path to the small harbor and approach a handsome, relatively new-looking sailboat, a huge fancy motor yacht and about three dozen other, mostly beat-up, boats of every description. All are tied up to a dockside slip at the edge of a fenced-in sheep farm and a couple of dozen weather-beaten storefronts that had clearly not seen paint since before JP was born.

In between baaaa's from behind the fence, Maddigan and JP look up at the dilapidated corner street sign, turn away and then quickly turn back for a second glimpse, then both laugh. The hand-lettering over faded blue says they are at the corner of "FLOCKING WAY" and "NO FLOCKING WAY."

"Hey, Mr. Rico," Maddigan says to the flap of the Jamaican's backpack, "Besides this funky intersection, where are we really? and"—shaking his head and looking puzzled—"...why'd you bring us here?"

"Funky! Yah, Mon. Like 'Funky see, funky do!' Ride? Yer still in Cosda Rica, Mon," he responds, bud I know anudder American here who owns dis big modor yachd boad. He be named Kummin. Lass name's Handy. Juss callum Handy is okay. God id?"

Maddigan and JP bite their gums to keep from laughing at how consciously they need to sort out and listen to each word their "guide" uses to mentally and selectively insert the letter "T" for Rico's use of "D" and consciously sort out those words that do, in fact, contain D's uh, not to be confused with 'these.'

"Anyway, all ya'godda do is say dad you be friends of Rico and maybe he helps you ged where you wanda ged. Yah?"

Rico looks to the sea as if it were a giant clock. "I godanoddhabuncha miles doo go before dark, Mon, so id's been nice knowin' yah boad an' ah wish yah well. Oh, and when Handy redurns here to his boad, leddum know where yah wanna go and he'll charge you somedin' and make 'arrangemends', if yah know whad I mean?"

"That's great, Rico," says JP. "Thank you for your help, your guide service and your company." Maddigan peels off two twenty-dollar bills from his waterproof passport wallet and tucks them quietly into the side pocket of Rico's backpack. "It's not much, Mr. Rico, but might score you some more smoke, yes?"

"No dowd aboud id," says a grinning Rico, as he turns to watch what he imagines his backpack pocket flap to be smiling at. "Andrew Jackson works good here also!"

"Well, we thank you!" Maddigan says. "By the way, that 'funky' quote of yours? It's 'Monkey' with an "M" as in: "Monkey see, Monkey do!'"

The Jamaican laughs and points to the street sign, "No Flocking Way, Mr. Rick!" then turns to walk away, chuckling to himself, but stops and turns back. "Oh, and MY 'by da way' doo YOU is diss: "Bargain da guy on his firsd offer. He always sdards oud with dollar signs in da eyeballs, Mon, especially if you're American, you know whadda mean?"

"Thanks, Rico," JP says, and hands him a tiny piece of paper with a quick-scribbled phone number, as he pats the Jamaican's shoulder. "Yeah," he adds, "and here's our number. "We appreciate your help. Anything we can do for you before we all get going?"

"Nah! Juss remember whad I look like in case I come doo see you bode in the middle of doze eighd million people and podholes, Mon!" All three of them laugh.

"Hey! You got it, Rico. Have a good trip!"

Rico gestures with a 'Thumbs Up,' the bright white of rolled joint paper prominent in the grasp of his dark hand, and struts away. Thunder rumbles in the distance.

Maddigan and JP scan the nearby dock full of tied up boats... a ramshackle collection of mostly beat-up old vessels ranging from the new sailboat and two other smaller ones, to half a dozen motor launches (only two look seaworthy), a couple of motor-mounted rowboats, and a dugout canoe next to the huge motor yacht.

Maddigan suddenly glances back to Rico, tells JP he'll be right back and sprints off to catch their walking-chimney-hike-leader.

"Hey, Rico!" The Jamaican turns. "Sorry to hold you up, but there's one more thing I meant to ask you: You know anything about a couple a fishermen who moved here from the States a few months back?"

"No, dare's doo guys moved here," he shrugs, "maybe dree-four munds ago. Dey muss live duegedder, bud dey be deep in da jungle and dey are sure nod fishermen."

"How do you know that?"

"Because dey come to down with differend modor boads, day are never duegedder, and needher seems to know much of anyding aboud whad's below deck, excepd dad id needs gas once in a while."

Rico takes a hit off his joint and turns away to exhale.

"Dey describe da land dey share da same way. One or da udder of dem comes here every doo-do-dree weeks doo buy food and supplies, excebd fish, and dey mead each udder here ad dah dock. Dey pay good so nobody bodders dem."

He takes two steps away, then stops and turns to say over his shoulder:

"Da word around here dough is dad day are definidely nod fishermen. Needer of dem knows da difference bedween a crawfish and a sand shark is whad I hear. I figure dey eidder ged dere nadive workers doo cadch dare fish. . . or dey maybe buy dem for dem. Know wadda mean?"

"Yes, Rico. I understand. Seems a little odd, If you should hear or think of anything else about that, please give us a call sometime at that number I gave you. Anyway, thanks again, Rico! Have a great day! Catch you on the rebound!"

They shake hands one last time.

"Yah, Mon. Da rebound," Rico's smiling as he turns. "Dad's for sure da place where to cadch s-duff . . . including good pod!"

Maddigan grins and heads back to JP who's sitting on the edge of the dock watching the boats gently rock with the tide change.

"Well," the Professor says: "He's definitely a character, but I think he was a sort of blessing in disguise for us, having met him as we did. And he certainly knows the area as well as the boat guys he suggests we meet. Wanna go check out that clothing store?"

Chapter 9

Catchin' stuff!

"Holy crap, FarOut! What the hell are we going to do when the boss finds out they got away? He'll have us cut up and fed to the sharks!"

"Chill out, Sauerkraut! Apple's behind bars so who's gonna tell 'em? Besides, we'll find them long before Apple ever even gets to his strudel. Ya knows what I mean?" FarOut smiles to himself when he realizes his Chill out, Sauerkraut rhyme and his Strudel pun were especially cleaver proof of what he calls his poetic nature.

"Okay, Boss, so you're so smart. Where do we start? This is a big jungle here."

"Don't be a wiseass, Wart!"—short for Willie Worrywart's last name. "Remember you are my assistant! Not the other way 'round! Now go get that launch kid and get the details from him on the boat they took," FarOut commands. "Uh, what details, Boss?"

"He's gonna know what direction they went and how much gas they had, and how reliable the boat is, and whether the launch had any food in it and—c'mon, you dummkopf, start acting like the detective you're being paid to be. And get the others cranked in. Remember, there's four of us and two of them. We got guns and they got zip! Find out everything you can and get back to me here. Quick! I'll hold down the fort in case they decide to come back. Now get going!"

"Oh! Hey! Wart!" FarOut calls out over his shoulder while lighting up the stub of his Cuban cigar knockoff he had earlier grabbed unnoticed from behind the pool bar and quickly snuggled into the corner of his flowered silk shirt pocket. "Be sure to check out that cruise ship that just docked here. Find out if anyone aboard noticed that pile of smoke I mentioned seeing this morning! I hear it was about sixty to seventy miles up the coast. It coulda been dem cookin' breakfast up on a campfire or somepin'—ya know what I mean?"

"Yeah, gotcha, Boss!" Worrywart walks off, nodding repeatedly left to right, as FarOut—rum and Coke in hand, cigar in mouth—strolls casually back to the topless honey at poolside.

Turning back, in a puff of noxious made-in-India cigarette smoke that drifted over the entire bar area, to the smiling bare-topped thong-bottomed female, Outtinger pulls a lounge chair up alongside hers. He waves to the pool bartender for two drinks, then fixes his lecherous gaze on the woman's breasts.

"Sooo, my dear beauty queen, how about we do these drinks I have coming over here for us to toast each other, and then we maybe take a little stroll to your cottage?"

"Y'know, I think that beach cottage we had before our boat-escape was pretty nice, Rick, did you? Too bad that jerk-excuse for a Fed Agent had to show up."

"Yeah, I agree, JP." He takes a deep breath as he looks around. "Well, here we are, at the intersection of FLOCKING WAY/NO FLOCKING WAY waiting on some dude named, if you can believe it, Kummin Handy, who we've never met, and who was referred to us by a

Jamaican pothead who we just met a few hours ago, listening to a bunch of flocking and no-flocking sheep baaaa at us while we get hungry and stand here needing a soap and water shower to de-crud our skin and be able to hug each other without feeling like two mudballs, or catchin' germ-stuff from our less-than-hygienic clothing." He takes another deep breath. "So, YES, I DO think we should check out that clothing store!"

She laughs. He laughs. They look each other up and down. "Yeah," she responds, "It's like Replacement Inventory Time for us in that clothing store, and you know, Professor, you're right! We could use a shower and some fresh dudds."

Realizing they may have to wait awhile for Kummin Handy, they begin meandering alongside the easy-breezy shifting waters at dockside, keeping within sight of what was maybe a million-dollar yacht called The Good Life in fancy gold script across the transom.

"Dah, dudds?" he questioned. Help yourself to dudds. I'm gettin' me some clothes. But thanks for letting me be right about something." He turns away and half-heartedly points. "Let's mosey our way over to the dudds place. We can still keep an eye on the boat from over there."

"Yah! Good idea! I definitely vote for food. Especially if it's packaged with a shower and some new duddsy-clothes. That little hotel across the way looks like a shirts and pants place connected to a café next to the entrance. We could get ourselves dudded and order some food, and see if they'll let us rent a room so we can shower and change. Maybe someone there even knows those not fishermen guys, y'think?"

"Y'think, JP? Where'd you get that 'Y' word? And duddsy? Maybe you should make your own dictionary? Give WEBSTER a run for his money? Wasn't y'think part of our Anchor Out counseling language when we lived aboard The Here & Now, before Solamenté's gang commandeered it for their upended drug deal, then destroyed it—not too shabby a vessel, our twin Daytona 400-horsepowered forty-footer…y'think?"

"Yeah, you think you're so smart, Professor, but I bet you don't know what I know."

"Okay, I give up…What do YOU know, JP?"

"I know that if I can't get a shower and fresh clothes with you before we eat, I might skip eating to get a swim with a piece of steel wool and a bar of soap, and grab a little fresh wool from those sheep over there to use for a cover-up!"

He laughs. "Yeah, well, I'd skip the 'steelwool-wooleybully' stuff if I were you. Steel-wool's not too great for your skin, and nobody likes a bully —even one that's wooley. Besides, you looked pretty good at the swim-up bar when you were all wet and soapy."

She smirks, and turns to head toward the marketplace. He joins in step. "Hey," she says, "when this Kummin guy gets back to his boat, and we tell him where we want to go, do we, uh, have any idea where we want to go?"

"Actually," Rick responds, "that's a pretty good question coming from a dirty, hungry, steelwool-scrubbing, marijuana-snorting boat thief with green eyes! The answer is, I guess, The Caribbean. We get there, we can figure out the next step."

"Gee, I'm so glad I asked. I never much thought of myself as a dirty hungry boat thief. Oh, and just for the record, marijuana isn't snorted—if anyone should know." She blinks and gives him a half-smiling one-eyed glare.

"Yeah, Babe. Slip of the nose, er, tongue! Sorry. Just tryin' to lighten things up a bit. I don't have any more idea about where we should be headed than you do. Someplace away from here, would be a good start." he says, feeling a bit distraught,

He continues trying to lighten the discussion. "The Caribbean opens more options to pursue than the Pacific unless, you're a long-distance surfer, or enjoy swimming with the sharks, or you love snakes, or you're piloting a freighter headed for New Jersey through the Panama Canal with 18,000 tons of hash from Colombia—"

She interrupts. "I don't think I'm interested in returning to that

Here & Now set of fiasco situations," she says. "So, okay, I'll opt for the Caribbean as long as you don't mind me tagging along..."

He puts his arm around her waist and hugs her toward him. Both grin. A sense of reassurance envelops them both as if it was oozing forth from the cheerful mariachi music pouring out of the café.

As they approach the building, they feel relieved to see the clothing store doorway and front wall displays of some decent-looking selections. They sniff some lip-smacking fragrances that flow from the stucco-walled kitchen. Three small children play in front of the hotel.

"Listen up!" Solamenté whispers to Guard Sanders: "You tell that contact of yours to let that asshole, FarOut, know if he don't catch them two this week, I'm sendin' a task force to hold him down while his pecker gets c-h-e-w-e-d off, and IF he recovers . . . "

"Gotcha, Boss," came the Guard's whisper between the bars. Solamenté continues: "Yeah, and one more thing: get word to the Seaport County Boss that I got a big-time ransom out for the 'Perfesser' and his broad—and to keep it quiet." The guard nods and moves on.

Chapter 10

So, Wazzup?

The top Guard knocks as he opens the door. "Wazzup, Sanders?" asks the Warden.

"Old man Apple wants me to threaten Outtinger, Warden. He says he's also puttin' out a secret reward for the Perfesser and his lady friend, and he wants me to get word to County Executive Wolferman. Whadda you want me to do?"

"Forget Wolferman! He's a clueless, retired half-ass professor and idiot politician, but tell Solamenté you got the word out on the reward. I'll take care of that. And I'll arrange a message to Outtinger myself. No need to get your feet in Solamenté's fire."

Sanders nods and turns to leave.

"Oh, and Sanders? Be careful. The man is harmless, but the company he keeps would slit your throat in an instant if they think you're baking the Apple—know what I mean?"

"Gotcha, Warden! Thanks." As Sanders exits, Warden Tantrumatto returns to his paperwork.

❧

Still-flopping fish wheel-barrowed across the dirt road from the newly-tied-up boat at the Plaza Dock and served with "flash-deep-fried" French fries than "taste so good they don't even seem possible to make, even by the French"bragged the owner and chef!

Maddigan and JP practically dive into their plates oiled with delicacies as the two fishermen boat captains, Kummin Handy and Kanger Rue step from the bar toward the couple's table.

"Hey!" one of them says with a friendly tone of voice and a big smile aimed at JP.

"Hey! Yourself! she responds with a smile in between bites.

"We heared," says the smaller of the two with an Australian accent, "you mates might be lookin' fer a boat trip, yes?" Maddigan responds: "Where'd you hear that?"

"The little lady who sold you each a shower and clothes says you're a nice couple interested in travel by sea."

"That might be correct," Maddigan responds, "And who is it that's askin'?" he says.

"This here's Captain Handy an' I'm Cap'n Rue. Kummin and Kanger be our first names. We have that 1981 eighty-foot Hatteras 4-Stateroom Motor Yacht across the way—The Good Life. He points. They all look.

Maddigan cuts to the chase. "Actually, we're looking for a quiet, scenic trip to the Caribbean, but we've already done enough flying and hiking to wear out the treads on our boots, as well as our energy pill supply. Plus we don't speak much Spanish."

JP picks up the pace. "So, if we were to rent the two of you and your boat and crew, what would you suggest as the best way to get from the slip you're tied up to across the street, to a nice vacation resort where we can just hang out and not have to deal with a lot of rowdy, loud, stumble-bum tourists?"

Cap'n Rue pulls a beat-up old map from his beat-up old jeans.

"Mind if we sit?" he asks politely while tipping his hat.

She gestures to the two empty seats at their table. Both sit.

"Well," he says, pointing a stubby little pencil point at the beat-up map he unfolds, "we could go north to Río San Juan. That river," he stabs the pencil stub, "runs along the Costa Rican border and connects the Southeastern tip of Nicaragua with the Caribbean."

Captain Handy nods as if on cue. "Or," Rue continues, "we could go farther north—all the way to the northern tip of Nicaragua where the Pacific spills into the Gulf of Fonseca—and then take Río Coco— that river's known as 'the Wanks,' by locals."

"Yeah," chimes in Handy. "The Wanks runs along the border with Honduras, past the Cordillera Isabelia Mountains with Mogotón Peak nearly 7,000 feet high all the way to the Caribbean." He waves his hand dismissively to underscore all the way, and then adds, "It's the longest river in Central America and, so, also the most dangerous to navigate—not to mention the weeks on the Wanks it can take to get from Ocean to Sea."

"Right, Mate," Rue continues, "then there's the Río Escondido which is a big-time transportation route between the Pacific and Caribbean coasts, but it's heavily-trafficked. Depends on what you're looking for, y'know?"

"If it was my call," says Captain Kummin Handy, who's clearly the senior of the two seafarers, and smart enough to have been watching the puzzled expressions on both JP and Maddigan's faces. "I'd opt for headin' South instead."

He points to his map. "We could take the Panama Canal and then cruise north along the Caribbean coast to a more tourist-friendly area —like Belize—some nice quiet resorts there, and the natives are very open and friendly. They don't even have electricity there yet, but they sure keep their Belikin beer cold!"

Maddigan laughs. "Yes, we don't know much about Belize electricity, but we do know a little something about that 'tough-to-break-Belikin-beer-bottle-glass!"

"That last option sounds best to me," JP says, over-riding Rick's comment to get to the point. She glances at Maddigan to see if he agrees. "Short and sweet," he says to her, and nods approval. "So," she continues, "What will it cost for that trip?"

"Well, let's see now," Captain Handy says, "we're lookin' at a coupla weeks there, a coupla weeks back, and a crew of three—a cook, a mechanic, and a deckhand—plus the two of us, and meals and dockage fees, and fuel, and any needed repairs, so I guess we're talkin' about somewhere around ninety-five hundred, but that's just a guess."

JP turns her plate 360 degrees and stabs another slab of fish with her fork. "Well, I guess you're not really interested in the adventure part of this trip, huh? Besides which, we're not looking to buy your boat, we just want to rent it," she says. Everyone smiles.

In between bites, she adds, "We'll cover all food, fuel and maintenance costs separately as long as you guarantee to use your best negotiating skills—which includes not winking at your suppliers!" She pauses and grins at them both, then continues: "So, with all expenses paid, I figure a thousand bucks for each of you and five hundred for each of the other three comes to thirty-five hundred—half up front, and half on arrival." She takes a giant bite of another fillet. "Mmmm, good fish! You want any?"

"Uh, no thank you Ma'am," says Handy. "Are you, uh, including alcohol in that 'all expenses paid' deal?"

"Well, I did say fuel, yes?" JP smiles. Maddigan smiles. Handy and Rue smile. They all shake hands. JP takes one last bite, goes to the counter and pays the bill with an extra tip.

"So, when are you ready to go? She asks the two Captains. They both smile. Rue looks at his watch.

Handy says, "However long it takes to cross the street and climb aboard!" They all head off together across the plaza, and climb aboard.

"Mind if I ask how you knew to look for us here?" questions Handy.

"It was Rico, as in Puerto, who recommended you," answers Maddigan. He said you were good guys and would help us find the vacation we need."

"Rico-as-in-Puerto. I'll be damned. Haven't seen him in months. Wazzup with him?"

"Well, HE is wazzup! Met him in the mountains; he hiked us here to FLOCKING WAY and NO FLOCKING WAY!" They laugh. "But he's a good guy!" JP adds. They agree.

JP and the Professor step aboard The Good Life. Rue shows them to the master stateroom and gives them a tour before they return to sprawl on the bed as the engines idle, preparing to slowly chug out of the slip and head for the gas dock.

JP pulls cash from the pocket of her brand-new shorts and counts out the 'half up front' she promised, along with her best guess amount for topping off the gas tank and a quick trip to the first alcohol supply source they can maneuver the boat to.

"So, wazzup with me?" she whispers to Maddigan, who's eyes have been totally fixated on her shorts.

"Hey!" he whispers back, "Me!"

She grunts and grins. They empty their backpacks, put their arms around each other, and the yacht sputters slowly up to marina gas pumps.

Chapter 11

Cut to the Chase

"But, Dean Oliviero, I've tried everything I can think of. I called their phone number; I drove to the cottage they had over on Laraine Avenue in Abbey Beach. I walked up the sand driveway. His Jeep was still there lookin' like the way he always keeps it, like new!" She takes a deep breath then continues:

"I knocked on the door and rang the bell. I rapped on the windows and even," her face flushed, "looked in the windows! The coffeepot was still plugged in and textbooks and some clothing and stuff was still kinda kerplunked around the kitchen and living room. I even contacted JP's lawyer/author-friend, Katie Didd, and she's not heard from them either."

"Thank you, Ms. Skender," Oliviero replies, "but we need to find him—them—check in with Chief Oleson, will you? See if he can track them down. If I can't reach Professor Maddigan, I can't even authorize architects to begin planning construction of the new Seaport County Community College Student Radio Station/Communications Center that Maddigan's proposed; plus: we need him to help us raise startup funds."

The Dean pauses and rubs his forehead briskly before continuing.

"And Dr. Barry, uh, President Davidson, who, as you know, replaced Andrew Moore Stafford on his retirement earlier in the year, is pushing me to get started with contractor bids because he likes the idea, and so does our Board of Directors. And, well, so do I of course! Trouble is there're no funds available to start with, and I think Professor Maddigan has some ideas about that!"

He picks up his unlighted pipe and gestures with it. "Turn over all the stones, will you please, Ms. Skender? If it helps move things forward, I don't care what you tell anyone. Tell 'em you're a special agent of SCCC.—whatever works—even if you have to tell people that you are the Dean." Both smile at the knowingly-exaggerated suggestion.

He pauses. He stands and walks her to his office door.

"Yes, I'm aware of President Davidson's desires," she says.

He smiles and nods before adding, "We really need to find these two people like lickity-split, y'know?"

"Yes, Dean Oliviero. I'll do everything I can over this weekend and let you know what I find out Monday morning—or sooner if possible."

"Good. Thank you, Ms. Skender. Oh, and say hello for me to your husband, will you? Uh—remind me of his name again?"

"Fender, Dean. Like the guitar. It's Fender Skender!"

He responds. "Uh, Right, yes—Fender," he responds. She smiles. He smiles.

"Ah, Yes, now I remember," the Dean says as he bites his gums to keep from laughing. "Well, thank you again!" he says.

She smiles, nods, and leaves. Seconds after she closes the door, he laughs out loud as he lights his pipe. "And she," he says to himself, "looked in their windows too! Imagine that!" he says, laughing in between pipe puffs.

"And Fender Skender!? HA! HA! HA! His laughing nearly chokes him as he spills out his last gulp of tobacco smoke!

❧

"This is nuts, FarOut! We ain't found nuttin' here. The kid with the boat swears he saw them headin' Nort' toward Nicaragua—maybe even Belize," he says. "He's got nuttin' to gain by BS'ing us, so maybe we should be headin' that way—like today?"

"Get the other two guys, get a car for the airport at the front desk—and be sure the bills are all paid. Meet at the lobby entrance—But hustle! We need to get there before the professor and his honey do," Outtinger responds (then lowers his head to hide his grin, having amused himself with his "honey-do / honey-dew" play on words. "ASAP, Kraut!" he calls threateningly after his assistant who turned to walk toward the office.

Discouraged that he'll have to leave bare-chested, thong-bottomed Michelle at pool-side, and blow out of the resort before sunrise, he scolds himself.

"If only I hadn't gotten so wasted yesterday that I couldn't find her room last night." He heads for the lobby and waiting car with his "team" of three bone-crushing dolts.

The three anxiously wait for Outtinger at the front desk. He arrives.

"Hear anything from the Boss?" one of them asks, as they all start walking out the lobby entrance. Outtinger nods.

"Yeah, the kid lied to us, but we got no time to deal with him right now," he says in a disgusted tone of voice as he steps into the resort's minibus. Solamenté's goon called the desk," he adds.

He then turns, looks over his seat back and waves a pointed finger at the three fake-agents. "So, we gotta go North to find these two slime-balls tomorrow or we got trouble. And We, by the way, means you!" He points to each. "And I don't need to tell you what that means." He takes a deep breath. "Move it, Mr. Rob Boyd!" he says reading the dashboard-posted driver's name.

As the Wagoneer picks up speed, Outtinger turns back again to look at his had-too-much-rum team and admonish them. But instead of telling them what he really thinks, he simply suggests: "You can sleep on the plane," as he tightens his seat belt and turns back to look out the front window, smiling with thoughts of "Poolside Michelle."

Chapter 12

A time to kill, a time to heal

From Solamenté to Outtinger to JP and the Professor: life and living—to each of them—means taking the right turns at the right time But none of them truly seem to fit in the right clock or the right calendar as two months pass.

JP and Maddigan and the "escape boat" crew almost lose track of their respective missions during month number one. The more the crew became connected with The Professor and his Boss Lady, the longer and slower the journey became.

Waiting on them hand and foot in exchange for cash, booze, company and paying the bills—like gas and tie-up site fees at each marina stop-off—all four of them honored JP's rules, but developed stop-offs as much as possible. After all, they were getting paid, plus plenty of free booze, and the chance to experience one plush resort after another —rooms, towns, opportunities, beach front swimming, room service, great food; cheerful, smiling resort staffers—a life none of them ever imagined.

And, in return, they granted JP and The Professor 100% privacy and a genuinely appreciative your-wish-is-our-command- attitude.

-They travel leisurely to the south stopping often on the way to Panama, keeping a reasonable distance between themselves—the crew was happy to be getting paid and having free booze all along the way, stopping every day or two at some plush resort that JP paid for—including meals, gas and overnight dockage fees, plus a few one-night stand girlfriends for the crew members, and a few minor boat repairs.

They end up stocking the boat with food, fuel, booze before departing from the northern-most tip of South America's mainland at Punta Gallinas to cross the Caribbean and end up a few days later in Spanish-speaking Santo Domingo in the Dominican Republic.

They tied up at the first dock they saw, just east of Puerto Rico and west of Cuba and Haiti. JP and Maddigan thanked and hugged each crew member, and paid them all the other half of their fees to get back to No Flocking Way Harbor, but speculated that having tasted the good life, the five of them might just decide to stay right where they were.

JP and Maddigan rented a car and headed inland and cross country to the upscale beach front resorts that lined Port Antonio's North shore. They huddled often along the way to consult the little English and Spanish Dictionary they purchased at the car rental office to figure out road signs, food ordering, and pesos. They eventually found and booked an oceanfront room in Puerto Plata with a balcony overlooking the North Atlantic Ocean. It was, in fact, on the map, in an almost straight line South from Seaport County and the Jersey Shore, which in reality, seemed a zillion miles away.

Now came the time to settle in and make decisions. First on the list is whether Maddigan should contact the college. His reluctance, of course, was tied to pressures related to having to lie or disclose where they were and how they got there and who was pursuing them and why. And of course, the bigger question was how did they actually get where they are, and in reality, who in fact was pursuing them and why. How credible could Maddigan possibly sound that they didn't have either answer?

All that hubbub and confusion dominates every thought, even in the playfulness of their relationship. Even on the crest of every wave, every mile of every day, the questions: "Why?" and "Who?" And the only answers either of them could bring to the surface were: Is there really, as the great song says: *A time for every purpose under heaven?* Is now that time? Is this the right moment for us to—again, as the song says— turn, turn, turn or do we just put our heads down and keep charging forward?

"Y'know, Professor Rick, I can't help but think that this *is* the season that the Byrd's song was focused on. We have enough money to buy back a respectable existence, and keep moving forward in life. It just maybe isn't what we once imagined, or the kind of existence we ever even might have considered, but that doesn't mean it's a wrong direction, or that it won't work."

Maddigan listens intently as she continues.

"I mean what if we just decided to buy or build a waterfront guest house in Rhode Island or Cape Cod or Cape May, and simply settle down and run the place? We could even offer classes for vacationers kinda stuff? Whaddayathink?"

"I think we should think more about your vacationers kinda stuff as we head to bed," he says, grinning, "and see what we wake up with in the morning." She grins back.

Chapter 13

Rain, rain, go away!

It's been raining downpours nonstop for three days and nights. The razor-wire- enclosed courtyard is flooded. All prisoners have been confined to their cells. Everyone is edgy-antsy. Heavily-guarded exercise walks inside the prison block halls with no talking have been permitted for some with lesser charges. Apple Solamenté is pacing in his 6x6 foot cell. Bo Strangles is pacing in his 6x6 foot cell.

Chop Sooey is standing in his 6x6 foot cell, clutching two of the three vertical steel bars in his 12-inch square brick-walled cell window. He is jabbering in Chinese. Phil Thee has been granted approval with three other prisoners to exit his 6x6 foot cell for a with two armed guards accompanying him and with his hands cuffed behind his back. No talking whatsoever is allowed during the thirty minute walk through prison block halls.

A friend of Phil Thee's who is also on the walk, suddenly goes bonkers into a non-stop coughing spell. No one seems to connect the fact that it occurs at exactly the location of Chop Sooey's cell. The hallway clamber prompts Sooey to stop gripping the window bars and to silence his Chinese chatter as he moves to the cell's hallway bars.

Thee abruptly backs up as he's pushed out of the way by one of the guards who rushes to Thee's coughing friend. This prompts Thee to stagger backwards up against Sooey's cell bars as Sooey quickly grabs a small folded piece of paper from Thee's sleight of hand offer to take it. Coughing subsides and order is restored, Chop Sooey returns to his window bars as prisoners are led back to their cells.

Ten minutes of quiet. The halls are empty. The usual level of chatter between cells resumes, and Sooey carefully opens the rolled up paper. It's from Solamenté. Sooey squints his one evil eye as he reads the note. The Boss is angry at his weak designated fake agent, Outtinger, and wants arrangements made to feed him to the 'Peckerbite' dog and decide on a replacement who will find the two escapee lovers and deliver them to slaughter.

Solamenté wants Bo, Chop, and Phil to put the word out to their connections that they each need to rally all their individual contacts to pull out all the stops and simply find this couple he labels as renegades who, he declares, have crossed up the organization. Once they're located, Solamenté says he'll take it from there.

His message concludes with the carefully worded threat that *"These two people and anyone who assists them deserves to understand that jail cells do not limit the ability to punish those guilty of double-crossing anyone in our family."* He goes on to say:

"I fully expect each of you who get this note (or a direct verbal version of the message) will marshal forces to pursue the ends of what is required in order to provide the long-term protection of our family and family interests, at all levels.

"You will further be expected to report any and all efforts to resist following the requests so that those circumstances can be dealt with separately, and thoroughly.

"You will keep me informed of any and all progress in this matter, and

of any information that will lead to knowledge of location and timing that can boost our odds for success. Start with a focus on the Caribbean and US West Coast!

"You will communicate and backtrack your way through the connections you are aware of and not share what you learn with anyone else. It takes only one weak response to this Family Protection Plan to collapse the goal and find yourself in a difficult position for yourself as well as your own family and friends. That I can promise!"

☙◦❧

"I can't even imagine where all this is headed," said FBI Agent Randy 'Red' Robbins. "Just look at this mess: No one knows where anyone else is. No one knows where anyone else is going. Neither the gang leaders nor the prospective survivors! And *we* are expected to figure this all out and take decisive action, so let's show 'em, what we got?"

Heads nod. The door to the FBI Team Case Study Room opens abruptly.

"Hey Red! Sorry to interrupt your meeting, but we just got a call from Seaport County College, Dean Oliviero, and he says he needs to meet with you ASAP. Something about some missing professor. He said it was urgent!"

Robbins excuses himself, has his top guy take over the meeting, then calls the County Police Chief, John Oleson.

"Hey, John. Can you grab one of your top guys and hop over to SPCC right away for an urgent meeting with me and the College Dean?"

☙◦❧

"Absolutely, Red. Me and Axe will be at the Dean's office within thirty minutes," Oleson says. "I know you guys don't often call local cops for help, and vice versa, but after this session with the Dean, we could really use your expertise and connections."

"I'm on the way, Chief! Maybe we can huddle at the diner after seeing the Dean."

Chapter 14

Puerto Plata Partner Platter

"So, JP, whaddaya think about all this adventure now that we're settled back down on the ground with all four of our feet?"

"Talk about your own feet there, Professor. Being as we are right now spending a third of each day bicycling back and forth to and in this heavenly town of Puerto Plata, combined with walking another third of the day nonstop through miles of sand along this beautiful ocean-front, and then swimming a third of each day kicking and ankle-bending through and into ocean waves—whew!—my answer is that both of my feet are starting to feel like flip-flops!"

"Jeeze, JP! Your three-thirds of feet activity doesn't leave any room for playing footsy at night!"

She smiles at him continuing with her word-play game.

"Well, Professor," she fakes a pout, "at night, in bed, there's plenty we can play with besides feet!" She grins and steps into his outstretched arms. "C'mon, let's head for the patio for some dinner. Then we can come back up here to our playpen, er, sorry, I meant our bed!"

They both laugh and head for the stairway to the outdoor dining area.

A Waiter greets them as they descend down the steps to the beach front dining area.

"Buenos Noches, Senior, Senorita!" He nods to each of them. "Habla Español?"

Maddigan responds with his thumb and forefinger squeezed together. "Uno Paquito," he says. The waiter laughed, but understood the misapplied intent.

He showed them to a table set off to the side, facing the spotlighted ocean waves. As Maddigan pulled a chair out for JP, a voice from the dark-cornered table behind them asked demurely, "Excuse me, but are you a professor from New Jersey?"

But for JP's quick grasp of his forearm, Maddigan practically fell over backwards. "Uh," he fumbled for an answer with a forced smile and managed to ask, "Who wants to know?"

"Oh, I'm sorry; I didn't mean to be intrusive. You just looked familiar." She and her companion both smiled. I just thought you looked like our son's favorite professor who started the student radio station with him as manager. We saw photos of the—"

Looking instantly relaxed, Maddigan took a couple of steps toward the couple's table. Maddigan cut her off.

"You're Royston Flude's mother?" Maddigan asked.

She nodded. He took a deep breath of relief and offered a huge smile as he reached for her handshake as he gestured to JP to join them. They all introduced themselves, romanticized versions of their common ground campus news, and shared news about the couple's son who was Maddigan's prize student. JP and Maddigan learned that no one in the campus-buzz circles seemed to have any clue about Maddigan and JP's situation. Rumors were that he and JP had headed for Cape Cod or Niagara Falls for the summer. The four of them ended up laughing about that and eating dinner together.

JP paid the bill and they accepted Royston Flude Sr. and his wife Florence's invitation to treat them the following night. JP and Maddigan headed back up to their room with considerable apprehension, but some sense of relief at the back-home news that the Fludes shared.

But neither one could sleep.

Bumping into that couple raised some consciousness, and prompted awareness that they were not as obscure and covered as they thought they'd made themselves. So, the night that each thought was to be anxiety-relieving and offer a great chance to get some sleep, turned out instead to be tumultuously awakening after having been suddenly recognized so far from home.

"Rick, the question here is if and how far we can trust them with knowing what led us here and what continues to feel like an ongoing threat— like I saw your nerves jumping when she asked who you were."

JP paused to collect her thoughts and then express her real concerns.

"Look, Rick, I know you don't like it any better than I do, but at some point, we are going to have to trust somebody with our secret. And if people like that can pop up anywhere and know one or both of us, how likely is it that those intent on finding us will succeed? Solamenté may be in prison, but it seems he still has enough control to unleash characters like FarOut to find us and kill or torture us or— Dear God!—both!"

"I know, JP. I feel the same way you do about this, but I don't know who to trust or where to turn. I know for sure I would not have survived another few weeks on that boat with those drunken vultures."

"What? Rick, you never told me that. I thought I was the only one thinking those thoughts. Why didn't you tell me before now?"

"You must be kidding, JP. It was bad enough that I felt that way.

I didn't want to turn you upside-down too."

"Well, as I'm sure you can imagine, I feel pretty upside-down now. So Whadda we do?"

"Uh—get rightside-up?" They both laugh and hug, then kiss.

"Mummmmmpf !!!"

Chapter 15

Rightside Up!

"So, JP, with all that's behind us now coming back to be in front of us, it looks like it may be time for a better plan than the wing-it one we've been following, y'think?"

"I do, Rick. I do indeed! Like it's time to start calling you Rick, instead of Professor, and it's time to decide what we're going to do from here forward. Y'know, we blew a few thousand dollars on that boat and the crew and all the meals and booze. But you're right that something's gotta change for us going forward because we can't continue to spend money like it grows on trees if we're going to actually end up with something at the end of the trail, y'know?"

"You're right, JP! We may never get chance to take in as much money again all at one time. Uh, by the way, just to be sure you know I am committed here. We add up all that's been spent and deduct it from the total of what we both got and then split what remains—just in case you thought that all that you spent was coming out of your pocket alone."

"Thanks for saying that Rick, but I never dreamed you'd walk away."

"As my father used to say, we need enough to invest for down the road, and have enough left over to enjoy life without having to struggle for every penny. Y'know, like, I'm sure you don't want to be a waitress for the rest of your life; you didn't take my classes for that. But if we don't end up with enough to live on, there won't be time to find the kinds of jobs that allow us to invest our skills and instincts without the threat of going broke along the way."

Nodding in agreement, she picks up on his emphasis and direction.

"And YOU," she punctuates her monologue with a foot stomp, "YOU need to find the situation that makes the best of your skills too. Personally, I think the direction we were heading long before this whole disaster occurred and before we actually had any money beyond seeding our fund for boat repairs and maintenance—and boat crew alcohol!—was—and still is—the right one. Uh, probably not the alcohol part." She smirks.

He picks up on her comments and ideas. "The point is so much has changed since then, but what probably has changed for the better for both of us is that those Anchor Out personal growth coaching sessions we ran on The Here And Now were big time successful, and I think we should focus one hundred percent of our energy on branding that program."

She circles the room then adds: "Yup, and those were just Saturday sessions with a handful of your students, but we could easily fill group sessions three or four times a week!"

"Maybe even five or six times a week?"

They both smile at the thought.

"Yes," he continues, "we can open our sessions to people not connected with the college who need to help themselves and their families) We can target small and family business owners and operators by helping them cultivate their entrepreneurial instincts, and help develop their skills and pursuits—in groups AND one-on-one!"

She responds, "YES! We can slowly raise our rates to market level—even set up follow-up sessions in a living room setting—maybe run a couple of morning or night deals as well." She pauses. "Uh, we may want to get some additional certifications?"

He nods and responds, "You're right about that, M'lady! And as we grow, we'll hire an administrative assistant to do all the paperwork, set appointments, and handle all the session needs—like ordering food and beverages, notepads, follow-ups, managing office expenses, setting up slide presentations—all that kinda stuff."

They both pause and stretch and take deep breaths. Both suddenly remember at that moment that there wasn't much of anything they could do for themselves until they could first figure out how to deal with the enemy and eliminate the threats that sent the two of them off to the Caribbean in the first place.

"You know, Green Eyes," says Maddigan, "we really do have to defeat these—pardon me—bastards—before we can make any of these other ideas reality. And that defeat has to happen fairly soon, so we can stop being on the run here, or we're not going to have any money left and we'll never be able to give birth to these great ideas."

He pauses and paces. "As things stand, we can't even count on the college for any kind of support or guidance. And how in God's name do we ever deal with this crooked underworld connection that runs not only through prison walls, but even impacts life events—as we've learned the hard way—far beyond America's borders?"

"No doubt about that!" she says. "So, we put first things first," she adds, right foot out, chin raised, arms folded, and looking defiantly over the tops of her glasses.

He grins. "Y'know, when you do that tough-guy stance, JP, all I can think of is I'm glad we're on the same team."

She smirks. He laughs. Then like a light switch, they both turn back to serious.

"So," he summarizes, "this seems like the right time to do an Action Plan."

They sit at the table. He pulls two notepads out of the desk set they've lugged around since rushing from their beach cottage for the dockside launch boat parked with its engine running at the resort. They each grab a pen and pad and start to write.

Chapter 16

The Plan is a Map

Daily beach talk-walks are capped by riding waves and wading through ankle-deep waves that sprawl across the sand at water's edge. The only interruptions are snack bar visits at the beach restaurant and, by doing homework with the various maps they've collected. And then —most importantly—by putting together a range of strategies that they are non-stop discussing, evaluating, hypothesizing, and frowning about.

It's midday. They stop about half a mile past the resort they're staying in and head for a small snack-bar about a hundred feet up hill in the sand. Piño Coladas and a shrimp salad with two forks. They find two deck chairs under a neighboring palm tree.

"Y'know, Rick, the more we talk this out, the less confident I feel about any of these *what if* plans we've been kicking around."

"Yeah, you're right. I agree. The problem is we can hardly take a breath without having some idea of where we need to end up. I mean, even if we're able to get these bastards out of our lives, where will our lives be? And what will they be? Are we going to be hunted down for as long as we live, and how long can we, will we, live? It's like a never ending jigsaw puzzle, and we don't have all the pieces."

He sips his drink and pulls a large shrimp out of it's shell, dips it in the cup of sauce, chomps on it.

"Well," she responds, "I'm glad you said that because I was beginning to think I was alone with that thought."

She sips her drink and follows his shrimp shell routine. There is silence as they look out over the water, then at each other.

"Like, will I ever see my family again? Will you ever reconnect with the college? Will we always have to be looking over our shoulders?

"We need a map, JP!"

She puts her drink and dish next to his on the small folding table between their two chairs and looks at him like he's crazy.

"Are you nuts, Rick? A MAP? What we need is to get the hell outta here, like W-A-Y outta here! Our vacation ended the minute that Farley asshole cornered us that day we took off in the resort's motor launch. How we even got this far without getting our asses kicked is miraculous all by itself." She takes a deep breath. "So, what's with the map? What kinda map you talking about?"

She continues without waiting for Maddigan's answer. "I mean, part of my family came to the United States from Holland. Y'think we should go there? Or maybe that's not far enough for Farley! Didn't you tell me once that your father's family came here from Armenia? Where the hell is that? Think we should go there? We have maps up the gazoo: West Indies, Belize, Dominican Republic, The Galapagos Islands, Bonaire. You name it! Oh yeah, and Costa Rica where we started our vacation." Arms crossed, she stomps her foot and glares at him over her sunglasses.

Maddigan's really tempted to laugh, but knows better. "Listen, JP: I am just as upset as you are, but we've got to put all that away for now and get focused on what it is that we need to do, and when, and how we're going to do it. Getting upset and ranting doesn't accomplish anything except raise our blood pressure. Let's be reassured at this point that we have what it takes to get the hell out of here, and out of all this stress. If you'll join me in taking a few deep breaths, that alone will start us out on the right road to the right place. Can we do that? Like now?"

She nods reluctantly. They stand, take a dozen deep breaths each and end up smiling at one another. They hug.

"Okay," says Maddigan. "So, I hear what you're saying and the time is now for us to put on our thinking caps and talk through where we think we are, and what we think we need to do, and where we think we need to go next, and how we're going to get there, and then most important, where the hell is it that we want to end up?"

"Y'think?" she says, smiling at all his 'thinks' as she gives him another hug.

He grins at her. "In other words," he continues, "A map is our PLAN! What's our end goal or objective? When we have that, we have a target—which is something of a moving target—which is a good thing because it always needs to stay flexible enough to be able to adjust it depending on circumstances—just like finding Mr. Rico and that 'No Flocking Way' boat and crew—and we need to remind each other that the frequent deep breathing helps us to go with that flow."

"Yeah," JP responds, "go with the flow instead of having to stop in the glop!" Both of them smile at the spontaneous rhyme.

"Oh, Rick, I know you're right. Sorry I lost it there for a minute, but the bottom line is that I just want to be with you—and all this other stuff keeps getting in the way—and it scares me that the wrong person—like Solamenté or Outtinger or one of their idiot honchos—is going to find us, and there would be no second chances. Y'know what I mean?"

"Absolutely!"

A long pause is followed by another sip and wrapping the remaining shrimp in napkins to take back to their room with their three-quarter-filled glasses of Piño Coladas.

Chapter 17

Ring! Ring! Yikes! It's the Room Phone!

A rude two in the morning awakening and quick scary thoughts occur to them both.

JP whispers, "Who knows we're here?"

Maddigan shrugs at her. "Hola!"

He holds the phone out so JP can hear too.

A vaguely familiar muffled voice: "Is this Maddigan and JP?"

Maddigan answers, "Who's Calling?" as he and JP exchange worried, puzzled looks.

The voice on the other end says, "It's me. Professor—Cap'n Handy. I musta called a dozen resorts lookin' for you and JP. Glad to finally get you. How are you both?"

Maddigan and JP both appear relieved, but puzzled.

Maddigan replies, "Uh, we're good, Cap'n Handy. So, what's up? You and the crew, OK?"

"Yeah, I'm fine," Handy responds. "The boys are fine. It's just that I got a call from some dude, says his name is—if you can believe it—"Filthy," and that he was callin' on behalf of someone named "Solomentality" or sometin' like that an' he wanted to know if me or my boys knew either of you. I said no because he sounded weird and there was a lotta static on the line. He didn't sound like he was all there, you know what I mean? Not drunk. Just like missin' a few brain cell pieces or sometin' Y'know?"

JP is visibly shaken. Maddigan gives himself a couple of wake-up pats on each cheek. "Is that it, Cap'n? Did he say anything else?"

"Naw. He just sounded like some coocoo, y'know? He blabbered on about some guy named Outonjur or sompin'. He told me the boys finished him off 'cuz he didn't do his job and started to warn me that that could happen to me and my crew too if we didn't help him find you two. I don't wanna get mixed up in stuff like this, Professor. Ya' know what I mean? So, I just told him I don't know nothin' an' my crew don't neither, that we'd been out at sea for over a month and just tied up at a marina and were headed for some drinks and to bug off and go take a hike! And I hung up on him, but I thought you might wanna know about the call. So, anyway, glad I got you. Please give our best — me an' the crew—to JP—and you have the number to get me anytime you need, night or day! Have a good night and travel safe!"

"Well, thanks Capt'n. I'll be sure to tell JP and I'm sure she'll join me in saying thank you for looking out for us. There's a lotta weird people out there, so it's good to know there are friends like you and your crew we can count on."

He takes a deep breath before closing the call.

"You take care of yourselves and please give our best to your boys. I have your number and will connect somewhere later on."

They both chuckle.

"Ah, to touch base and so I can send you guys a couple of bottles for partying. Take care, and thanks very much for trackin' us down and makin' this call!"

"You bet, Professor. And me and the boys will look forward to hearing from you and the boss-lady once you're settled. Tell her hello for us, and both of you take care also, and remember to call anytime you might need us again!" *Click!*

"Oh, my God, Rick. Who the hell is this filthy guy and how did they know to try to connect with the boat captain and crew? And what if this call was a set-up?"

"I understand the skepticism, JP, but these guys were always square with us and we just have to trust they'll not be sending anyone our way. We did, after all, treat them right and paid 'em what was a small fortune to them, right? So, let's not get paranoid."

Taking a deep breath, JP says, "You're right as always, Professor."

She pauses and looks around the room, regains eye-contact, and takes another deep breath. "Now, about that cuddle position we were in before the phone rang?" They hug, close their eyes, and promptly fall asleep.

At seven there's a knock on the door and a voice calls out, "Breakfast is now being served downstairs!"

The two of them rub and open their eyes. Both grunt, hug, kiss and take turns heading for the bathroom. JP first.

Once they're both awake, into their bathing suits, sweatshirts and flip-flops, they head down the stairs and find a table and chairs in the sand that's set apart from the main dining area. Breakfast is a help-yourself buffet with more than twice the amount of food that all resort tenants combined could possibly eat. They load their plates. A waiter brings them coffee. Crashing waves roll a hundred feet down the slope. Guitar music. They eat quietly, exchanging stares at one another, and the ocean.

Coffee refills arrive as their empty plates are removed.

"Y'know? I could get used to this," she says, scanning the horizon with intermittent looks at Maddigan. "It's just too bad that we'd never be completely relaxed knowing what could be the bad guys walkin' along the beach here in front of us—or sitting at the next table." They each give a casual, yet suspicious, glimpse at the three men at the next table.

"I've been thinkin' about that Map Plan idea of yours, Rick, and it sure makes a lot more sense than no plan, y'know?" He nods. They finish their coffee and head back to their room.

Chapter 18

They Map the Plan

"First of all," Maddigan summarizes, "we have no way of knowing who these creeps are or where they are. Only that the Boss is in a maximum-security prison, or at least that's what we were told. Anyway, we have to map out a plan that is very flexible depending on the latest, input we get as we move forward."

He looks to JP to see her response. She nods agreeably. As he paces slowly around the room. He glances out the sliding doors to the deck, facing the sunlit ocean.

"So," he continues, "if we head, now just for example, to Western Canada and learn that whoever's pursuing us is in Vancouver, Washington, we need to be able to switch gears and immediately head for Florida, or Bermuda, or Ireland, or—"

"Armenia!" JP chimes in, attempting to hold in the accompanying grin. Maddigan laughs out loud, then collects himself.

"Right, JP, Armenia! Seriously, though," he continues, "the bottom line is that we're going to have to develop some kind of ongoing, hidden system of communications that allows us to always stay one step ahead!" He takes a deep breath, "and I'm not really sure what that system is or needs to be, but we're gonna have to come up with a way to get started. Any ideas?"

She starts to frown and nods slightly as she answers him.

"Well, I'm not sure either, Rick, but maybe we need to find someone who gets it and does know how to help us get through this mess. I mean it would certainly be a better investment than buying forty million bottles of booze for a boat captain and his crew."

She smiles momentarily when she realizes what she just said, but quickly returns to her stern-faced look.

"I mean it seems to me that our best investment—with this pile of money we got—is to spend some of it to pay for guidance and protection, y'think?"

"Now that's a good point. In fact, it sounds like a plan, JP. I just wish we had a better fix on Solamenté's communication channel. We know next to nothing about who he communicates with, or how—y'know?"

He strokes his beard and continues. "Like does he have just that Outtinger guy and his so-called team, or are there other groups like them floating around the planet? And how do they get Solamenté's orders if the guy's in prison? On top of which, I got the impression he was in a solitary confinement situation except for a couple a short courtyard visits once in a while when there's good weather. And what do they actually know about us and where we've been and where we're headed and—"

She interrupts his flow. "Oh, Rick, I don't know how we could ever find all that out. But you're right. It really is frustrating, and worse—it's scary! Somehow, we have to figure it all out if we're going to survive, and if we're going to end up with any reward money left when this is all over if we do survive. I wish I could—"

He interrupts, "Listen, JP, I agree but we need to stay focused on where we go and what we do going forward." He rubs her shoulder gently. "Bottom line is that all the information we have is all the information we have and we may never find out more!" He stares pensively through the glass slider out to the sea, and continues. "So we have to decide what we do going forward." He pauses, and rubs his forehead as if the answer will pop out.

"Well," she says, trying to bring a smile to his face, "if you're talking about a totally different, maybe more obscure place, maybe we could just drive to Florida and hop onto a spaceship and go to the Moon!"

She smiles nervously. He smirks.

Her smile fades quickly. "Whadda you smirking at?" she says. "I didn't say you should go to Florida and throw me a moon!" Her grin surfaces again! "I just thought it was a kinda spacey idea." She finishes the grin with a question mark. "Y'know?"

"I understand what I think is you're kidding, Green Eyes. But let's get serious here. I mean, are you suggesting we should go someplace that's really far away. I mean bottom line is that we can't just keep running away forever, y'know?"

They pause to ponder in silence. After a couple of minutes of silence, he picks up the conversation again.

"Do we, for example, get surgery to change how we look? I mean, who does that kind of procedure? And it's not likely it could be undone, and how safe is it anyway? Or, do we hire our own detective to dig up information, and do we need a different kind of detective to implement what we find out and—"

She stands and cringes at the thought. He picks up on her voice and body language and tries to appease her.

"Babe, I wish I were Superman, but I'm not, and all I can do is keep thinking and trying out ideas with you and hoping we are able to stumble onto some revelations that take the stress away and allow us to just be ourselves and not always having to look over our shoulders. The problem is we haven't a clue about what to be looking over our shoulders for—or at!"

He opens the glass-slider and steps slowly out to the balcony. He appears to look to the water for answers. She watches. They both instinctively take deep breaths at the same time.

"I've been thinking about something," he says, turning himself and his attention back to face her. She's remained seated on one of the room's canvas deck chairs, six feet away inside their room. She sits up.

"Maybe I need to step up," he says to her, "and take the chance of having a heart-to-heart telephone call with the Dean. Maybe he has the right connections to help us get out of this mess. The thing is that I run the risk of losing my job when he hears the whole story."

Maddigan slaps the deck rail alongside the glass-slider.

"Well, I can truly appreciate that concern, Rick," she says. "But the bottom line is that we need to survive first. Then worry about where we end up and where you teach. There's always a place for you on this planet to teach others all the life lessons and skills you share as a professor. And all that we've been through and have worried about doesn't make a damn bit of difference when it comes to your teaching skills *or*, when it comes to our abilities to run our Anchor Outs."

She pauses and stands. She takes two steps toward him, and looks up into his eyes.

"In fact," she says with a sense of conviction, "this whole terrible experience could turn into a great learning experience for us to share with others who feel hopeless and confused. We'll be able to show them that even the worst of times can produce a positive experience and results that matter."

She turns away, then back to face him. "And, after all, isn't that what we're supposed to be doing to help those who come to our sessions? Why would we not apply it to ourselves?"

She steps toward him and wraps her arms around him. He responds as if just awakened from a nightmarish sleep.

"JP, you are the best! You know that, don't you? Let's take this discussion for a walk on the beach, and maybe the answers we've been looking for will roll in on a wave. Y'think?"

"Uh, yeah, I do think on occasion. In fact, I think there's something we need to do right now, before we go for that walk."

Maddigan smiles and responds: "But, JP, I thought we'd wait 'til after dinner to, you know—fool around!"

She laughs and whispers, "You dingbat, I was just gonna suggest we grab our hats and sunglasses." Then she whispers even lower: "But after dinner will be great, Professor!"

They both laugh and hug, take their hats and sunglasses, and hold hands as they head for the stairs and the sand.

Chapter 19

Whaddaya mean "I dunno?"

Over a week of bad storms forcing twenty-four-seven confine-ment to their six-foot square cells served only to exacerbate already edgy bad moods, bad ideas, and bad behaviors in Solamenté's Solitary prison cell bloc.

Reduced to bitching, moaning, complaining and throwing stuff, all three of Solamenté's confidants—Bo Strangles, Phil Thee and Chop Sooey—were each at their wit's end. Being squashed for space behind steel bars was bad enough, but not even having a few minutes to talk with each other and—of course—with Boss Solamenté in the court-yard felt demeaning, discouraging, disillusioning and just plain shitty.

The sum total of their outside world connection was reduced to a couple of hours of static-filled portable radio broadcasts that filled the cell block halls from six to seven in the morning and from midnight to 1 in the wee hours. The morning broadcasts were religious services and the midnight programming was filled with farm skill instruction pro-grams that ranged from how to milk a cow to how to collect chicken eggs and how to shovel horseshit—great stuff to know just in case any listeners in solitary ever get out of jail and need to find work.

Day number ten of confinement finally brought some sunshine and respectable temperatures. Inmates were fit-to-be-tied as the Warden explained in a series of Reminder Meetings he held with each cell block group of guards. Some short visits to the Courtyard would be allowed but they needed to be riot-ready and have quick access to their guns and gas masks if necessary.

∿•∾

Solamenté, Thee, Bo Strangles and Chop Sooey were all huddled together in the prison courtyard for the first clear-weather-day break in what seemed to each of them like forever. Fewer prisoners were allowed at any one time in the courtyard at long last filled with sunshine. They sat quietly together.

"I dunno, Boss . . . "

"Whaddaya mean you dunno?" Solamenté whispered loudly as he squinted and clamped his lips together in a show of frustration. He looked around at the walls, the guards, the small groups scattered about, the younger guys playing basketball.

Phil Thee responds in a whisper to Solamenté's question, "I only know that they took a long ride on a fishing boat converted to a cabin cruiser, but can't get any straight   answers about who, what, when, where, if'n y'know what I mean? I still got guys who're checkin' for details, but nothin' yet."

Thee looked like someone had just stabbed him. He thought about making excuses, but then, instead, simply nodded shamefully to Solamenté.

"Sorry, Boss! There are some things I just can't control and, being in here, I don't have the clout I used to be able to use to make things happen to get the answers I need to the questions I ask. Ya' know what I mean?"

Solamenté looked at Thee over the tops of his sunglasses.

"Yeah, I unnerstand, Phil. I know you ain't no Superman, but bottom line is I need to find these two and where they went and where they are." Solamenté slapped his leg as an exclamation point, then continued. "This is personal," he emphasized. "y'unnerstand?"

He coughed up some phlegm and spit it about an arm's length from Thee's feet, then continued.

"They were a good part of the reason why I'm here to start with. "Ya' gotta hear what I'm sayin' here. Outtinger couldn't make nothin' happen so he had to get lost there in the jungle, y'know what I mean? So pull out all the stops, okay?"

"You got it, Boss. I'll do everything I can."

Solamenté answered under his breath to himself, "You fookin' better do everything you can, asshole, or you ain't long for this prison." Thee's pocketed hands turned to fists as he got Solamenté's best fake smile.

Thee glanced around the Courtyard, thinking to himself, "Who does this son-of-a-bitch think he is to threaten me, anyway? One more comment like that, and I'll play his game on him. He thinks he's such hot shit. He can order all of us around and—"

The ear-shattering horn blew three times through the loudspeakers ending the courtyard visit time. All of them rose as the armed guards approached to escort them back to their cells.

Chapter 20

Now Where do we go?

"Once we're on the plane to Newark Airport, and get home for the weekend, and can find a way to get to Seaport County Community College, and you give up this heart-to-heart telephone thing you've squirmed around with, and simply get yourself in front of the Dean with like some big fat donation check for building the new Student Communications Center—you're not gonna have any problems."

Sounding miffed, Maddigan responds to her scolding. "Whaddaya mean not have any problems, JP?"

"Listen, Rick! The Dean will be ready to do anything, arrange any kind of protection from Solamenté's connections. We have got to start thinking more positively about this whole thing. Yes, there's no doubt that there are some Solamenté gangsters out there looking to beat us to a pulp and earn points with their asshole boss who's in prison for life, but the Dean has some snaggle of his own, and he's on the legal end of things. And, whatever you donate ain't no peanuts to this college. If you want to feel reassured, name the Communications Center after him!" She smiles.

"The point is," she continues, "that you've got to step up to the plate here. Now! You know that I'm with you one hundred percent, but we can't sit on our asses, or our thumbs any longer—or keep running for the rest of our lives. You have the Dean in your pocket, and this may be our only chance to get away from these Solamenté creeps. Here's the bottom line. Let's be thinking about what it is that we can do with what we have, not what we can't do with what we don't have, okay?"

He steps toward JP with the burst of a smile on his face, and hugs her. "You're right, Green Eyes, as always. *So* right! I don't know what I'd do without you."

"You'd be horny!" She laughs. He laughs. They hug again, and kiss. Mmmmmph! He grabs the phone and asks how to dial a number in "The States."

❧❧

"Dean Oliviero? This is Rick Maddigan. I—"

"Hey! Where y'been? We've had a task force here trying to find you. You Okay? And your friend, JP? Where are you? When are you coming back from vacation? What's—"

"Whoa there, Dean! Thanks for your concern; JP and I are both fine. We just needed to get away from all the clamber. I think I can get to your office beginning of next week. Do you have any time Monday morning?"

"Any time! Yes! *Any* time you can get here will be great! I'll move my schedule around. Monday? It's *your* call! I'll make myself available anytime that works for you!"

"Great! So, can I catch you at nine-thirty in the morning? Is that okay?"

"Nine-thirty it is, Rick; I look forward to seeing you then! Have a great weekend!

"You too, Dean. Thanks! See you Monday morning."

❧

Maddigan smiles at JP. "Well, I guess you were right. That *was* easy!"

"Of course I was right, Professor," she smiles. He doesn't know our personal-life situation, so he thinks he needs you more than you need him, and that leverage will get you what you want, so we need to talk some about the best ways to present yourself to him so he still thinks he needs us more than we need him as we head for the next step. Knowwhaddamean?"

"Absolute, JP, and that's not a request for vodka!" She grins at his response. "Also, I been thinkin' it's gonna be the perfect time to stop in and see your folks and little sisters who are also all off for the summer, and—" She rushes at him with hugs and kisses—just for the thought. They head for the front desk to pay for the room and meals and to make taxi, flight and car rental plans to, at, and from Newark Airport.

After forty-five minutes worth of arrangements, the desk clerk mentions casually, "Someone stopped by last night to inquire if you two were staying here, but we told them we never heard of you because some of our staff people told us they thought you were on your honeymoon and we never allow newlyweds to be interrupted here."

Maddigan smiles and quickly drops three ten-dollar bills on the counter. "Two of these for you and the other for whoever else was part of that exchange, like your front-desk person? Anyway, thank you, and—yes—it's been a great honeymoon!" JP grinned and nodded.

They climb into the airport taxi and look at each other with a big "Whew!"

Chapter 21

RE-mapping the Plan

Though they found themselves looking over and past each other's shoulders before, during, and after boarding their flight to Newark, travel was happily uneventful.

"I never thought I'd be glad to be going, of all places, to Newark, New Jersey. I mean, talk about gangsters! Has it occurred to you that Newark has always been a breeding ground for the Outtinger's and Solamenté's of the world? At least that's always been the conviction of my family and all our Jersey Shore neighbors while I was growing up, and even most people at the College, and I think—"

"JP!" Maddigan interrupted, "I've always thought that too! I mean my brother and I were the poor kids in a rich town north of New York City. Actually, at the time, it was the second richest town in the whole United States, behind, uh—Beverley Hills!"

"Yeah, Rick, you told me that. What does that have to do with gangsters?"

"Well, it doesn't really, but in those days, we thought it did. We grew up in a tiny third floor walk-up apartment on top of a little candy and newspaper store and a little grocery store next to the train-to-New-York-City railroad tracks.

"Our building's back alley was like the town's hidden slum. Our father was always double-checking to make sure no one had let down the fire escape ladder—which was only for in case of fire, but was sometimes lowered as a prank by kids that lived above us. Dad worried because of what he called riffraff people hanging out in the alley—drinking, smoking, and yelling curse words—which, of course, Dad did him-self every day—and smashing empty booze bottles thirty feet under our kitchen window.

"We always joked that since the kitchen was only five by fifteen feet with a lumpy, crooked-floor tiles, a thirty-inch walkway between the sink, stove, cabinet, dinky kitchen table, and dumbwaiter on one side, and the refrigerator, cabinets, and space for two squished table chairs on the opposite side. We weren't too worried about anybody really big trying to climb through that back end fire-escape access window, and actually walk the tiled floor walkway to get to the fifteen by twenty foot living room. Whoops! Sorry for the diversion." Maddigan took a deep breath pause. "Bottom line is what that flashback represented."

"Here's the point," he continued. "I've had many instances in life of distancing myself from gangsters—or befriending them when there was no other reasonable option. And I did this for two different reasons. One, because my business career in New York and New Jersey was literally surrounded by Mafia connections, and two, because they scared the hell out of me when they started talking about meeting objectives and satisfying needs, and wasting people who didn't agree with them. And interpreting their grumbly threats—assessing the meanings behind the words—was always unnerving to me."

Their stewardess arrived, smiled, and took their lunch and beverage orders. Two tuna salads with chips and two glasses of Chardonnay.

JP half-whispered to Maddigan, "No match for piŋo coladas in coconuts with fresh pineapple, but, y'know Chardonnay's the only white wine with the same anti-oxidant heart-protection values as red wine. And I'm happy to be going home, for you to see the Dean and for us to see my family!"

"Absolute!" replied Maddigan. "Yeah," she whispered with a smart-aleck smile, "but 'Absolute'? There you go with that vodka salute again!" They chuckle and cuddle. "Happy Saturday, Professor!"

Thirty minutes later came a short announcement from the pilot urging stewardesses to collect all remaining food, beverages, and wrappers, and passengers to put their seats and tray-tables in an upright position and make sure seat belts are snug because there were minor turbulence reports heading into Newark Airport.

҈

"Listen up, you asshole! Farley Outtinger was no prize performer, but the short time he spent as a private eye gave him a one-up over our other gophers at that level. At least he could play a convincing cop role," Phil Thee whispered aggressively to Chop Sooey during the latest prison courtyard break with Solamenté and Bo Strangles.

"All right, you two," Solamenté interceded, "Yeah, Outtinger was okay for what he did before, but not this time." He looked around to make sure no one outside their foursome was listening. "This time he screwed up bad and deserved to get chewed up bad," chuckling to himself at his Outtinger-style *screwed up/chewed up* rhyme.

He quickly returned to his tough-guy demeaner with stern, squinched-eyes.

"Bottom line is we still ain't got what we want and nobody knows nuttin' about where those two disappeared to." He slapped his right fist loudly into his left palm. A dozen nearby heads turned, then quickly turned away, after discerning Solamenté as the source.

"We gotta figure they're still somewhere in the Caribbean gettin' drunk and screwin' around on some beach—OR…" He looks both ways and covers his mouth with his hand. "OR sometime soon," he whispers, "they gonna be comin' home to Mama, ya' know whadd-ahmean?"

He slaps Bo's thigh and slowly starts to stand as he whispers, "So tell me tomorrow who we know can check out their home base comings and goings—y'know? Family? Friends?—and keep us posted. I'm gonna have a chat with the Warden here sometime time in the next coupla days." He looks around as he stands and stretches. The 'Clear The Courtyard' whistle blows and the guards start lining up at the building entrance.

☙⚭❧

"Oh, my God, Rick! Were these last three months for real? Maybe we're just imagining it all." He nods to her, but is preoccupied with what he sees as he pulls the Newark Airport rental car into their Jersey Shore Abbey Beach cottage driveway on Laraine Avenue.

He rolls up to the chain, puts the car in Park, and strolls nervously to the chain to put his birth date into the combination padlock, returns to the rental car and drives it over twenty feet of hard sand to park alongside his Jeep, which hadn't moved an inch but had four flat tires.

"Shit!" he mumbles and stomps his foot as he sees the flat tires and then sees the razor-sliced canvas top and seat covers. He slaps the rollbar. "Dammit!"

"Wazzup?" JP calls to him from the rental car. He points to the tires and canvas.

She jumps out of the rental and scurries up to him with a hug and soft words. "Oh, shit! I'm so sorry, Rick! I can't even imagine how you must feel." She stays in the hug, takes some deep breaths with him, then speaks softly, "But we have to stay focused on our purpose here and accept that there's nothing we can do about this today—except check out the cottage inside and try to find Axe, the lookout guy we hired to be staying next door with his eyes on our property." He nods and loosens the hug.

"C'mon Rick! Let's get our stuff out of the rental car and get inside. Hopefully, everything's okay in there and your hired guy is just napping or on a beach stroll. C'mon! Let's get our stuff and check out the cottage. Then we can look for our guard guy and go from there, y'think?"

"Yup!" he says quietly. They return to the rental car and collect their three pieces of luggage, turn to face the cottage and, still holding hands, walk quietly together to the front door. He takes the spare key he's carried with him for the past three months out of his wallet and opens the front door.

❧⚘❧

Without a single word spoken, Solamenté looks both ways as all cell lights go out. He passes his prison section hallway guard a small envelope with a hand-drawn apple over the sealed flap. It's addressed: "PRIVATE To The Warden." The guard smiles at the apple, tucks the envelope in his shirt and walks away.

Chapter 22

Sounds Like a Plan

JP and Maddigan see the cottage appears to be undisturbed at first glance. Stuff has collected dust. Nothing appears to have been moved or removed. Even the electric clock shows the right time, so no apparent outages while they were gone. JP gets a dial tone when she lifts the phone.

"Well, first glance," he says, "all looks okay here, JP. How about you keep checking stuff out while I hop next door to see if our retired-cop house watcher is there and find out what he has to say about the Jeep?"

"Sounds like a plan," she says as she continues to take mental inventory and move their luggage to the bedroom.

"Yeah, a plan." He follows her lead and goes out the door, heading diagonally toward the adjacent cottage, shaking his head as he passes the Jeep. He hears their phone ring behind him and makes a mental note to remember to check with JP about the call when he gets back.

He approaches the front step of the neighboring cottage and is just about to knock when the door opens. it's Seaport County P.D. retired Lieutenant Douglas Axel.

"Well, welcome home Professor! Glad to see you back. How was your vacation?"

"Good to see you too, Axe. We had a once-in-a-lifetime trip," replies Maddigan. "It was pretty amazing. How about you? Looks like you did a good job of watchin' the cottage, but what happened to my Jeep?"

"Honest to God, I don't know. I took a walk up the street to the beach last night. It was supposed to be one of those super low ebb tides we hear about that only happen once in a while, y'know? It was super low all right. Seemed like a football field distance to the waves that are usually almost up to the road, y'know?"

Maddigan nods.

"Anyway," Axe continues, "when I got back—I wasn't gone more than twenty minutes—I saw a dark Ford pickup—no lights on—kickin' up sand, racin' out of your driveway, onto the road, and turnin' left off Laraine Avenue onto the main drag out there."

He points. "Y'know—Route 35, headed South. I hustled down the street to check out your cottage which seemed untouched, but then I saw the Jeep tires all flat and the canvas and seat covers torn. I checked for foot or tire tracks too but last night's wind and rain musta blurred them all out!" He scowled. "Got a rental car comin' here in the morning at seven. County Police Department's coverin' the expense. Anyway, "I called our Desk Sergeant and filed a report, and they came out to take pictures early this morning. But they've had no reports of any kind about this area since. In fact, I just checked again about an hour ago—nothin.'"

Maddigan looked distraught. He paced slowly as he listened.

"At least whoever it was never got into your cottage. I'm sorry about what happened, but it was the only time I ever left this place without calling in for a backup 'cause it was so stormy and I was only walkin' fifty, sixty yards up to the beach and back," he lamented. "I only stayed on the sand at the edge of the road for ten minutes!" He took a deep breath. "I mean I even called in a backup every week just to go get some groceries—which makes me think whoever it was, was watchin' the place. I mean how would they know I was here, and then that I walked up the street to the beach? Y'know what I mean? Like the person or persons who did the damage did it all in just a few minutes and then split before I got back. Good thing I wasn't gone longer."

Maddigan stood still absorbing the input, then walked four steps to the window reassuring himself that the view to his and JP's cottage was clear and unobstructed.

Then Axe spoke up again. "I'm really sorry about the Jeep, but I made sure to file a report so your insurance company will have some substance to justify paying your repair and tire replacement expenses. In cases like this, I know they'll take care of everything pronto!"

Someone knocked on the door.

"That must be JP, Axe!" Maddigan says as he turns and opens the door.

"Welcome home, JP," Axe says.

She looks unnerved as she smiles and nods. "Good to see you, Axe!"

Maddigan summarizes what Axe was just saying about what he thinks happened to the Jeep. He stops in mid-sentence. "You look upset. You okay?"

"Oh, Rick, I just answered the phone and a voice said, 'You an' yer old man better watch yer asses and get back outta town quick if ya' know what's good for you!' And then he hung up! It was not any voice I recognized." She stepped to Rick for a hug.

Maddigan turned to his retired police friend. "Whaddaya think, Axe? I mean I have an important appointment with the Dean tomorrow morning, so I'm really glad you've got a rental coming. I'm not sure what I would have done without a car!"

107

"You just go do your thing," Axe responds. "I'll stay here with JP, and you should know we have some backup hanging out in the other empty summer cottage on the opposite side of your driveway. I already made those arrangements before you got here, and I'm told they'll be here within the hour, and—"

JP interrupts: "Thank you, Axe, for all your help and attention. I'm really not sure yet if I will be in that meeting with the Dean or not, but if you and your officers will keep an eye on this house and ours, and the other empty one across from here, it will be greatly appreciated. Oh, and if Rick and I decide I should go with him in the morning or not, I'll let you know between 8 and 8:30. The meeting at the Dean's office is set for 9:30. Right now." She grabs Maddigan's arm. "We gotta get some shuteye cause we're both pooped and our flight into Newark was a bit bumpy. So, thank you for all you're doing to help us."

"No problem. I hope you both get a good sleep! See you in the morning," Axe says as he turns and walks away.

They leave and walk up the adjoining driveway, shaking their heads as they pass the Jeep, then stumble into their cottage and bedroom, set the alarm, and crash into their pillows. She never mentioned the second phone call. It was just ten words of warning from the same voice. "By the way, the Dean ain't gonna help you none!"

❧❧

The alarm went off at 6:30. JP and Maddigan literally crawled out of bed.

"Ugh," Maddigan groaned, "not enough sleep. Can we re-set the alarm, maybe grab another hour?"

Her face had a parental-scolding look.

"Not on your life, Professor! You gotta be super alert for Dean Oliviero, unless you're ready to dump everything we know and everything that's happened into his lap. You told me this would be a very important meeting and that we couldn't afford to have him know the truth about what we've been through because it could open other doors that you don't want—"

He cut her off. "Yes, JP! You're right, as always. If I am ever to remain on the faculty there, it would not be in our best interests to share what's been going on all summer. The Dean's totally trustworthy, but others in the Administration and some idiot faculty members—who I've heard feel that I threaten their careers with my open classroom style—would badger him endlessly for more information that—misunderstood or misrepresented—could end up designating me as a big threat to the College's name and reputation.

"It is, after all, a community college underwritten in part by community funding. So, let's think this through after we get cleaned up and dressed. And, yes! I believe it will help for you to be in the meeting. Let's get going here and then we'll put some ideas together about how we explain certain experiences, y'think?"

"Sounds like a plan, Professor! See ya' après-showers 'n shaving 'n toothbrushing. Whoever finishes first fixes the coffee. Deal?"

"Deal!" he says, as they rushed to the two small separate bathrooms.

Both emerged at almost the same time and grabbed two mugs of coffee along with notebooks as they left, snarling as they passed the Jeep. They checked in with Axe at 8:00 to get the rental car keys and let him know they were leaving and would stop in as soon as they returned. Axe wished them a successful meeting and watched them drive away,

At almost the same moment, his two fellow officers arrived in an unmarked car and parked behind the cottage opposite Axe's, separated by the slightly longer driveway that housed Maddigan's Jeep. One of them entered that cottage while the other moved quickly to Axe's door and stepped inside. All was quiet, but a sense of edginess hung in the air.

Chapter 23

APPLE Cider, Sider, Slider juice

"Whaddayamean, they got the Jeep, but never got into their house? What the hell is that supposed to mean?"

"Listen, Apple, this ain't no easy task here. Bottom line is they got police guys livin' next door, watchin' the place twenty-four-seven, y'know what I mean? So, gettin' the Jeep was all they could do and they almost got caught doin' that. So, bottom line is we gonna hafta wait 'til just the right moment wit no cops around."

Phil Thee pauses, looks around to inventory Guard locations, then summarizes. "At least we finally got the S.O.B.'s on our radar after all this travelin' all over the Caribbean time, know what I mean?"

Solamenté takes a deep breath and rubs his forehead.

"Listen, Phil," Apple responds, "You know when and how to pull the strings, y'know what I mean? And I trust you and Bo and Chop to figure this out."

Solamenté bends down to adjust his socks and quickly look left and right for Guard locations. "At least we finally know where they are, so as long as we keep 'em in our sites, it's just a matter of time 'til they slip or slide and we can waste 'em. There's still plenty of our boys out there who will do what they're told, so we just gotta do like the old Solamenté expression: Take The Time To Drink The Apple Cider, right?"

"Right, Boss," Thee responded, "and we're all better off if we take our time and do this thing the right way with nobody gettin' found out, know what I mean? Besides, you gettin' even, and not gettin' found out means we can get scumbags like these two again and again! It's like we're settin' up a whole new system to manage from right here and throw the switch whenever one of our six-by-six cellmates livin' here inside is lookin' to get even with someone or some group on the outside, and don't want nothin' traced back."

"Phil's right, Apple," Bo chimes in. "I seen plenny'a times over the years guys like you or me, or Phil or Chop, here, would give up their middle finger to make arrangements to be able to eliminate somebody on the outside, y'know? Like especially somebody who squealed on him or convinced others he was guilty when maybe he wasn't or maybe only a little bit, y'know?"

He pauses to look behind the bench they're on, then continues: "I mean once you're in the Big House here, ain't nothin' y'all can do except survive, never mind get even. Ask Phil here 'bout that. He's been stuck here longer than any of us."

Chop Sooey has been listening intently. He nods agreement emphatically and adds, "Yup! No way to be an Apple Slider here!"

"Okay, boys," says Solamenté. "I hear what you sayin' and so all of what I'll need from you is to help me get this job done." He pauses to rub his hands together, then brushes back his whiskers. Then with a half-grin, he adds, "And every time anyone in this fookin' place asks what you want to drink, forget milk or coffee and order Apple Cider —or Apple Juice if there's no cider. *Then*, toast the four of us! Got it?" They all smile and nod.

Thee raises his paper cup of water. "Toast to our four-man team of Apple Siders."

The deafening back-to-your-cell horn blows, vibrating through the walled-in "courtyard." They stand and walk slowly through the dozens of other prisoners toward the guards at the hallway entrance... visions of "success" with their newly energized team and purpose, as visions of toasting each other with apple cider, dance in their heads.

❧

"Katie Didde? It's JP!"

"*OMG*, for real? How *are* you? *Where* are you? What's going on?"

"Well, let's see. Yes, I *am* for real! I *am fine*. I *am* back *home*. But the what's going on question might cost me more of a phone bill than I can afford, and I'd have to sleep somewhere in between answers. I'd *love* to see you, and find out what you've been up to besides your law firm clients! When can we get together?"

"Tomorrow morning?"

"Sorry, Rick and I have an important meeting with SPCC's Dean. How's dinner tomorrow night at The OceanFront Steakhouse? My treat?"

"WOW! Great! How's six o'clock?"

"I'll make the reservations the minute we hang up. I can't wait to see you. How's 5:59pm?" They both laugh.

"See you then—with bells on!"

❧

"Here's to us!" JP clicks her glass of apple juice with Maddigan's as they sit in a booth at the College Diner. They are half a mile east of Seaport County Community College's main entrance, en route to a meeting with the Dean of Instruction in an hour and a half. Both have their second cups of coffee—after those they brought from home for their ride to the diner—and plates full of bacon and eggs with home fries and toast.

"Y'think we deserve a toast?" Maddigan asks, reaching for slice of toast with a grin and his glass still raised post-click.

112

"Yes, Professor!" She smiles at his toast. "Because we are about to ensure your return to the classroom and recruit the Dean to join with Axe and his support team in protecting our interests and—"

"Shhhhh!" He puts a finger to his nose and lips as he nods toward an older couple in the booth across the aisle who appear to be listening! She peeks sideways in an instant of awareness.

"Whoops! Sorry." she whispers in response.

As they finish up and get ready to leave for the campus, Maddigan tucks a three by five file card—filled with notes made during breakfast—into his shirt pocket, pretending—as JP suggested—that the Dean meeting should be treated as a class presentation.

"And that," she emphasizes, "means that your key points should be itemized on the card to make sure nothing important gets accidentally overlooked."

Minutes later, they enter the campus archway and head for the faculty parking lot. As they get out of the car two of Maddigan's students, who were walking past headed for early semester registration at the Administration Building, stopped to say hello. One asked where his Jeep was. "Getting a tune-up," he responded with a smile. They nodded and let him know they were registering for another of his classes in the new semester.

"Well, thanks," he said. "I look forward to having you both in my advanced class." Maddigan smiled. JP smiled. The two students smiled, then headed off for the ground floor registration room.

Maddigan and JP joined the walk with a dozen other students to the Administration Building, then took the elevator by themselves two flights up to the Dean's office.

Just before the elevator door opens, JP squeezes Maddigan's hand, and says "I love you!"

He grins ear-to-ear as they step off and he whispers back, "I love you too, JP." They head down the hall to the Dean's Office.

Because they had at last produced a viable and productive strategy for presenting information to Dean Oliviero—a persuasive thought process to share with him that they are convinced he surely will accept and take ownership for—and which they believe is *great* because it takes them out of the spotlight—and the Dean, who loves attention, can step up to the proverbial plate wielding a *big* bat!

"Y'know, Rick," JP says, "I think we got ourselves the making of a really great plan here that will work for all of us. For you, me, my family, the dean, the college, the county, the State, the prison system, and decent people everywhere who are being taken advantage of by prisoners who are supposed to be being punished for having taken advantage of and interfering with the lives of people who are honest, respectable citizens to start with. *Whew!*" she adds, "that's a long sentence, but I know you get it!"

The elevator door opens. They step out and look at each other.

"I get it indeed, JP. You just said it all, and I couldn't agree more."

So much had happened already, in their minds—just since Katie's call, and then clinking their juice glasses—and now...

Chapter 24

The Dean Make the Scene

Niceties exchanged with Marguerite, the Dean's secretary, ended with, "Well, let me take you right in. I know he's very anxious to see you both."

Pleasantries, back pats and handshakes exchanged, they sit at a small round table at the Dean's floor-to-ceiling library wall opposite his sun-lit, window-backed desk.

Marguerite brings a tray of coffee, three donuts, milk and sugar to the table, lifts the coffee pot with a smile, pours the three cups and leaves, closing the door behind her.

"So, tell me where you two have been?" says the Dean, "and, where are you now, and where are you headed?"

Maddigan sips at the coffee as he pulls the note-filled three-by-five card that was clipped to the file folder he carried in, and glances at JP with the hint of a smile. "Well, "Maddigan begins, "we feel like we've been everywhere, and we are *at* the Dean's Office. The "Where we're headed" part? We are headed toward wanting to see that SPCC

Student Communications Center that we've talked about actually happen!"

Dean Oliviero tilts his head slightly as he leans forward toward them with a puzzled look on his face as Maddigan takes a deep breath.

Maddigan reaches into his shirt pocket for a small piece of folded paper and hands it to the Dean. Expecting some kind of secret message, the Dean adjusts his glasses, unfolds the paper and jumps up from his chair!

"*Oh my God, Rick!* is this *for real*? Are you *serious*? And *you, JP*— this is all about you too? *tell me you're not kidding here!*"

"No, Dean Oliviero; we're not kidding. It's like that brand of vodka, y'know? *Absolute!*" she says, giggling.

All three of them are smiling ear-to-ear.

"This check," says the Dean waving it nervously. "It's $175,000 for Seaport County Community College Student Communications Center construction to begin immediately." The Dean shakes his head and the check. "Is this for real?" he asks.

Maddigan and JP cannot stop smiling.

"The answer to your question," responds Maddigan, "is like JP just said: *Absolute!* One of the reasons we took so much time off and traveled was to decide how and when and how much would do the job. We came to an estimate that this would cover all the construction, tech equipment, soundproofing and furnishings, and we wanted to see it start now so that publicity could begin to encourage enrollment increases for the Fall."

"I'm stunned! I can't believe it! I've always known your heart was here on campus, Rick, and assumed JP's was as well, but I never even imagined you would be tapping into your reward money to fund this project and program. And this, he says, goes far beyond the SCC campus. It will benefit the whole county." He kept staring at the check.

"Well, we are hoping for exactly that, Dean," added JP, as Maddigan took advantage of the Dean's excitement to glance at his notes.

The Dean reached for his phone.

Maddigan held up his hand. "Wait, Dean, before you call anyone about this, please give us just a couple of minutes to explain some of what's been behind this decision and how you might be best able to help us with an immediate situation that needs to be addressed before depositing this check later today. We promise it won't bounce, by the way." Three huge grins fill the room!

"I'm all ears!" the Dean says.

"Thank you," Maddigan responds. "Here's the story. While JP and I were recovering from the confrontation that led to all of our upset and our need to get outta Dodge as they say in the movies, we decided to take advantage of having the summer off, having a pile of cash reward money, and wanting to visit some quiet, exotic, remote island resort to escape the clamber of news media people, the trauma of the experience itself, and the sudden surge of underhanded money-hungry gangster types."

He stopped to take a deep breath. JP, who'd been watching the Dean, gave Maddigan a quick reassuring wink with the eye that was out of the Dean's vision range, which stoked Maddigan's engine, and prompted a report of their travel details:

"We had only been gone a couple of days and ended up in this beautiful very remote island paradise on the West Coast of Costa Rica only to be confronted by one of the bad guys posing as a Jersey-based FBI agent who did everything short of just plain kidnapping us in an effort to take us back here and turn us over to undercover Mafia guys who worked for the Solamenté family so they could avenge their evil-doings that sucked us into this whole thing in the first place." Oliviero looked stunned.

"That started us on the run so to speak," JP says.

"We came back here because of you and this campus, and JP's family. We have learned, in just the last twenty-four hours, however, that we are still being pursued by some bad guys under Solamenté's control and under his New Jersey roof, so to speak." Maddigan pausesa moment to let that sink in, then continued.

"We have friends in local law enforcement here who are watching our Abbey Beach cottage as we sit here. Some extension of this evilness has already sidelined my Jeep and has apparently been stalking our residence."

A look of deep concern sweeps the Dean's face, as he's been listening intently.

Professor Maddigan gets up and walks contemplatively toward the window overlooking the campus. JP's and the Dean's eyes follow him.

He turns back to look at them. "We're not looking for you or the College to save our butts, Dean. We simply want help figuring out how to download the publicity and turn off the communications line from the California prison to the Seaport County community." Maddigan pauses. "Bottom line is that we need help in turning off the faucet that's feeding the local Mafia people here in Seaport County, who seem intent on chasing us down. And probably needless to say, we prefer to not have our names be mentioned here, or anywhere until Solamenté's communication channels and mafia authority are squashed. So, the bottom line is that for us to have you take this check on behalf of Seaport County Community College, we ask only that the project funding be treated as 100% anonymous until such time as this man, his authority, and his channels of communication are thoroughly silenced. Maddigan glances at JP. "And, of course, that includes protecting JP's family."

Quiet floods the room. He walks back to his chair and sits. But now the Dean stands as if it's Act II on the same stage, and walks to the window, then turns to face the two of them.

"This whole thing," he says, "just isn't right!"

He rubs his forehead vigorously. "There's no reason the two of you should have to undergo this tormenting, threatening treatment and I will initiate contact today—right now, this morning—with State Department of Education leaders.

"I'll get them to turn this mess around immediately. I will insist on finding the weak communication links that keep these illegal directives from prisoners flowing, and get them to put an end to this *today! Now!* From what I figure, we'll need to go far above the prison Warden level to connect and *dis*connect the pieces. I will *not* involve your names in any of this without your written and notarized permission."

He strokes his forehead, pulls his pipe and tobacco pouch out of his top drawer, puts them off to the side on top of his desk, paces back and forth a couple of times, then stands a moment looking out the window.

"In the meantime," he says as he turns back to face them, "stay in constant touch with the police people who are protecting you and your residence. Get your Jeep repaired immediately and bill me! I will see that the college pays for that. Above all, let's get your police friends here to provide equal but unseen and unspoken protection for JP's family starting today! I still have a couple-a hours before my noon meeting. Can you two stay here with me while we initiate these actions?"

Both nod positive responses.

The Dean buzzes Marguerite, who enters and clears the table as Maddigan wistfully eyes the departing untouched donuts. JP sees his forlorn expression and laughs to herself.

"Too late!" she scribbles on his notepad. He smirks, but vows to get one later.

"How about you two heat up your coffee and move yourselves to these more comfortable chairs by my desk?" the Dean asks.

The three of them refill their coffee cups, move toward the desk and sit. The Dean picks up his phone and makes a series of calls, explaining each call to JP and Maddigan in between.

☙❧

An hour later, they leave the Dean's office with more encouraging handshakes and back pats.

"You have my word," the Dean says, "I'll do whatever it takes to help untangle this mess and to create a successful groundbreaking and construction plan for the new Center. The two of you are a true blessing to this college, and I am proud to count you both as my friends."

Once they're both back out to the parking lot, they smile and climb into the rental car before risking an on-campus hug and kiss. No one sees them.

Chapter 25

Where JP Came From

JP opens the front door and Maddigan follows at her heels. Her Mom and Dad and two younger sisters—fourteen and six—are all in the kitchen chit-chatting while getting lunch together, and are exuberant, nearly hysterical when—after a whole summer of communication shut-down—the two of them walk into the kitchen unannounced.

"Oh. My God!" Hugs, kisses, back pats, smiles, grins, laughter.

JP's parents, Joan and Pete Haley, are both happily surprised — actually thrilled—to see them. JP's sisters, Pamela and Olee are practically doing somersaults! Ear-to-ear grins on every face.

Salad, sodas and sandwiches. Pretzels and chips. JP describes it as "Like having lunch in a beehive, with no stings of course, just lots of buzzing around!"

Maddigan recounts their travels, from Costa Rica to the Dominican Republic via a fully-staffed and equipped eighty-foot cabin cruiser. And JP, of course, chimes in her take on people and places that Maddigan described.

The Haley Family is mesmerized with the storytelling and thrilled with the unexpected visit. Endless questions. Entertaining answers. Smiles and laughs throughout.

"So, we're back home," JP finally summarizes after some ice cream and homemade chocolate chip cookies, "and it will take us a few days to get resettled. In fact, Rick's Jeep is in for servicing at the dealership; it got worn out sitting still all this time." She winked at Maddigan who was grinning ear-to-ear.

"But in another couple of weeks," she continues, "we should be all back to normal with class schedules and our Anchor Out sessions and hopefully, hopping back and forth to see y'all like my new Southern Islands accent?" Everyone smiles.

They excuse themselves mid-afternoon, blaming the tiresome travel hours, but pledge getting back to normal" with visits and phone calls. And with a smile, hug and nod to each sister, JP reassures all that she and Rick had not forgotten her two sisters' birthdays coming up next month—Pamela's fifteenth and Olee's seventh. Smiles all around.

The girls walk them out to the rental car. "So, Rick, where's your Jeep?" asks Pamela. "Getting a tune-up and weatherproof roof!"

"It should be done In a few days" he adds, "and you'll be the first ones to get a ride, uh," he looks quickly to JP, "after JP gets a ride, of course." They all grin.

"See y'all soon!" JP half-shouts, as Maddigan starts the rental car engine.

They head on home to their Abbey beach cottage, seven miles south. Halfway home, Maddigan turns to JP and says: "Y'know, we never said anything to them about staying alert. Let's call them when we get back, or first thing in the morning." She nods.

☙❧

Up until that moment, JP and Maddigan were both lost in quiet thoughts on the fifteen-minute drive back to their cottage. They looked forward to some quality "talk time" with "Axe," their newly-retired Seaport County Police Lieutenant neighbor for whom they'd rented the one-door-closer-to-their ocean roadside cottage so he could keep an eye on their home and belongings. They were also anxious to meet two of Axe's fellow special assignment officers, who were reportedly now hunkered down and out of view in what appeared to be an empty Laraine Avenue summer roadside cottage facing Axe's cottage. All had a perfect view of the Professor's four-flat-tires-and-sliced-seats-and-canvas-top Jeep.

As they pull into their driveway, Axe steps out his back door and walks toward the rental car. "Welcome Home!" he says as the couple steps out of the car. They both nod and smile.

"Hey Axe!" the Professor returns the greeting. JP is smiling. They all shake hands.

"How was your meeting?" Axe asked. "Great!" they respond in unison.

As they stretch and look around, JP is quick to share the news with Axe.

"The Dean was very receptive to Rick's plans for the college's new Communications Center, and of course a big chunk donation of our reward money for the construction."

"WOW! That's great!" Axe responds, smiles, then continues. "And while you were gone, we arranged to get the Jeep up the ramp onto a flatbed truck and off to the dealer's for new tires, seat covers, tune-up and new canvas top. Other than that, it's been super quiet. Only a couple of cars actually passed here on the way up to the beach—judging from the fishing gear and folding chairs attached to their bumpers, both looked like surf-caster types in search of some fresh dinners."

He looked directly at JP's non-stop smile. "I take it you had as good a visit with your family as you did with the Dean?"

"Yes indeed!" JP replies. "And thank you for asking. It was great to see my parents and sisters again after this long summer. And even though we only had time to have lunch together because we wanted to make sure to have some time to touch base with you, and the two men you've recruited to help, to work out some ideas. Thank you for asking. And thanks for taking care of Rick's Jeep!"

Laraine Avenue, usually packed with cars and people all summer, looks deserted.

"Let's talk inside," Maddigan opens his and JP's cottage door to invite Axe in, but stop and smile, "Um, Axe, would you mind getting your two officers to join the three of us here for just a couple of minutes? We'd appreciate the chance to meet them. No rush! JP needs to make a quick follow-up call to her family."

"Absolutely, Professor! Yeah! It'll be good for us to all be on the same page about this assignment. I'll go grab them both and be right back."

Chapter 26

Return to the Axe and Katie Didde

JP smiles as she hangs up the wall phone. Maddigan walks slowly to his E-Z Chair, looking forlorn, imagining having to take another big chunk of their reward money to fix the Jeep and thinking it best to not accept the Dean's offer to pay for repairs. He no sooner sits down and JP brings her smile to him.

"Well, they loved our visit, Rick. And Dad will keep them all on alert for now." She scans the room. "Everything looks in order and untouched since we left this morning. I'm anxious to know what Lieutenant Axe and his two buddies think about all this. I wonder if any of them know anything about the communication channels between prisoners, wardens, and Mafia people in this area."

"Yeah, me too, JP."

Three knocks sound at their door. JP opens it and ushers them in—no uniforms, but no doubts about the waist-side lumps they carry under their jackets. Axe does the introductions of Officers Mike Infusino and Ron Focazio.

"This," Axe says to his fellow officers, as he politely waves his arm sideways toward JP and Maddigan, "is the couple we are working for to help them avoid top prison security-breaker threats from a bad-news Mafia Don/Con—a guy who's been leading a quiet, hidden plan of assault from his solitary confinement, maximum-security, six-foot-square prison cell in California." Axe lets his opening comments set in, then continues.

"This creep, Apple Solamenté, has been able to—somehow or other—communicate freely with New Jersey mobsters and get them to stalk and threaten these two fine people, JP and Professor Rick Maddigan here, who, I assure you, you'd be proud to call family. JP and Professor Maddigan are tightly connected to the people and principals of Seaport County Community College, and this State that we've all grown up in."

Axe pauses as the four of them exchange smiles and handshakes, then continues: "You may have read or heard about them a few months ago when they succeeded in upending the Solamenté Mafia Regime here in Jersey. They won a handsome reward for all they suffered and beating the bad guys at their own game." He glances out the window at the disabled Jeep.

"These two heroes travelled almost twice as far away as Miami in search of some peace and quiet and the chance to finally breathe," he continues, "to try to regain some peace of mind from the evil confrontation Solamenté presented them with. Well, they were then mercilessly tracked by Solamenté mobsters through the Caribbean, repeatedly threatening and interrupting what was supposed to be their vacation!

They've returned here and to SPCC campus. And they're still being harassed!" Axe glances toward the window. "Evidence of that," he says, "is the damaged Jeep we'll be shortly loading onto a flatbed truck." He pauses to let that sink in. "Here's the bottom line. It's our job to protect and help them and to figure out how to short-circuit the Solamenté mob-rule threats so the two of them can get back to normal and

126

doing what they do best—helping other people!"

He steps dramatically toward the window and starts talking over his shoulder as he turns back to face his two officer buddies, and gestures a slight hand movement toward Rick and JP:

"These two have been helping our community, friends and family members to produce and gain more from life than any of us could possibly do. My brother was on one of their Anchor Out group boat trips."

Maddigan and JP had no knowledge of this and Axe's comment feels like a shot of adrenaline.

Axe looks at them both. "Yup! He returned like a new man. Told me they helped him get rid of his bad attitude problem, which I can assure you was genuine, *and* be a better father!"

Axe returns to the quick meeting's purpose. He looks at his two officers. "Whaddaya think Ron? Mike? This all make sense to you about what we gotta do here, and why it's worth some extra effort?"

Both officers nod their heads emphatically.

"Well, good. We're all on the same page," says Axe, "so let's put some *immediate* and *down-the-road-a-piece* ideas together, and allow JP and the Professor here to get some rest while the three of us come up with some kinda action plan for cutting these Mafioso slime ball communication channels."

They all smile. The three nod and shake hands again as they leave.

"Catch ya in the morning!" Maddigan calls after them. They nod and gesture a slight wave and salute.

As the three of them close the door and start walking together to Axe's cottage, JP looks lovingly at Maddigan and tries to summarize.

"Y'know, Rick, this has been one hell-of-a day, week, month, year!" She smiles.

They unpack their luggage in five minutes.

"Yup! I keep thinkin' about what you called a hell-of-a year, JP; you ain't kiddin. And I don't know about you, but I'm beat!"

She nods agreement, but then says: "I'm tired too, but I promised

6:00 o'clock dinner with Katie Didde at the Oceanfront Steakhouse, where we both used to waitress a few years back. I assume I can use the rental car? And you know, the restaurant's just down the road a coupla miles."

He nods, and says "Yup! Just be alert," and gives her the rental car keys.

"Hey! Yup to you too!" She laughs! I should be back by nine-thirty" she adds, "and I'll wake you up then, whether you like it or not."

He grins, and heads for the bedroom. As his head hits the pillow and—without even changing clothes—he kicks off his shoes, grabs the huge twin bed cover, and says, "Not to worry, JP. I'll like it just fine as long as you wake me up like slow and gentle."

She gives him a quick kiss, and he's asleep almost before his head hits the pillow.

She grins, says "Yup!" and tiptoes out.

੭৵৻

"*OMG*, JP, you are like textbook-tanned! You look stunning! And I am jealous!" They hug, exchange cheek-kisses, then settle into a quiet corner table, with already-poured glasses of Chardonnay." They each reach to quietly toast one another and take a sip.

"Well, I'll tell you, Katie," JP says, "it's been an adventure-filled summer, and I'm sorry I didn't call or write, but it was with good reason, which I'll explain, and I *do* have a gift for you."

Katie grins, takes another sip.

JP leans down to pull a carefully-wrapped, ribbon-bow-tied "To Katie" gift from her large purse and narrates, as Katie carefully unwraps the five-by-seven-inch, handmade, two-inch deep frame that fingers can reach into to touch each scene item.

"I thought of you when I saw it at an ocean beach art exhibit in the Dominican Republic. It was part of a 3-D original assortment of in-depth—hand-made of course—framed scenes. It looked like the kind of place I thought you might choose as a vacation beach cottage—all hand-made and complete with a woods surrounded by a sandy yard, topped with a tile roof, outdoor water-storage vases and even a small wagon for weekly market trips and excursions to collect driftwood."

"Oh, my God!" Katie responds with a huge grin. "It is exactly the kind of place I dream about one day owning and vacationing to—will you visit? You are too sweet! Thank you!"

The waiter arrives. they both order the same menu-featured steak dinner.

"So, Katie, tell me how your defense-case clients are doing?"

"Oh, all's well. I have a couple of interesting cases, but it's you who's been adventuring, and I'm more interested in hearing about you and Rick and your travels. We can catch up on my stuff anytime. Tell me while it's still fresh in your mind. Who'd you meet? Where'd you go? How was the traveling? Did you spend all your reward?"

They both laughed, realizing it would hardly be possible to spend it all at one time.

JP laughs as their appetizers arrive. "Well, I'd need a thousand hours to fill in all the gaps, never mind describing details, but here's the short version."

Two hours later, they agree to finish the story next week. They cheek-kiss, hug and head home.

Chapter 27

The 3:00am Threat

Their immediate sleep is ushered in by feeling relieved and reassured that Axe, Ron, and Mike would be alternating sleep hours to provide full alert and that they are all camped out just a few strides away in both directions. Knowing that the Jeep is back to the dealership for repair—and that Dean Oliviero is jubilant and reassuring—meant that this might be their first uninterrupted night of sleep since they left their drunken boat crew in the Dominican Republic, a perfect stress reduction plan.

At least until their phone rings off the wall at 3:00am!

Maddigan jumps up, rubs his eyes and grabs the receiver as JP grunts and rolls over, back to sleep. Maddigan half-whispered, "Who's this?"

A gruff voice responds, "Never mind who's callin', asshole! This is just to let you know that we know where you are, that you got guards, that you met with the Dean after having breakfast at the diner and that then you went to your old lady's family's house, and that should be enough to keep you awake all night!" *Click*.

Afraid to wake JP, he whispers "Who is this? Who is this? Dammit!"

"Shit!" Maddigan whispers as he crawls back under the covers. The call is disturbing to say the least, but he isn't going to wake JP or call Axe.

If that guy knows all that he said, and is calling with a warning, he isn't going to be heading to their doorstep tonight. He's just trying to rattle our cage.

"Gives us something to deal with in the morning," he whispers to as he falls back asleep.

છ—જ

"Good job, Rocko!" says Solamenté. "The Warden came by middle of the night with his pocket tape recorder and headset for me to hear your message to this wise-ass couple, and recorded this message right now from me so he could play it back to you on his private phone. Bottom line is, make sure you followup. And let me know." *Click*.

છ—જ

Along with the 3:00am call message—just minutes after JP woke-up at 7:00am, splashes water on her face and sips some coffee—Maddigan says, "So, we need to connect asap with your family, JP, as well as with the Dean, and, especially now, with our police protection team. And," he adds, "we need to do this today—*now!* Okay?"

"Well, what's so urgent?" she asks, still feeling groggy. "Did you have bad dreams? When we went to bed, everything was fine. So, what's this all about?"

"No, Babe. No crazy dreams." he responds. "Just an evil phone call, but I didn't want to wake you for that, especially considering how tired we both were, and that we are well-guarded right now, y'know?"

"Okay, so what was the phone call? Who was it? How long did you talk? What was the subject raised? How did—"

131

"The call was a threat! I have no idea who it was. I never got to talk. It was like one long sentence and a hang-up! The guy's voice was gruff and nasty and his words were threatening. He seemed to know more than I would have guessed possible considering the circumstances, and my main take-away response is that we need to meet with our cop-guards here first thing this morning because the bad guys seem to have a bead on your family as well as us—so we want to make sure your family is protected too, without having to explain too much to them, and starting immediately, like, before we begin to worry about putting a plan in place and taking any pro-active stance!"

"Oh, my God, Rick! The guy threatened my family ? Who was he? What do we do now? We should call my father immediately? I—"

"No, JP, wait! We don't want your folks to panic! We want them to be alert, and for our guard-team to add a couple more guys to their lineup who can look after your whole family ASAP! *We* need to stay calm and in control, take active steps toward identifying the caller and toward briefing your family in a reassuring way. Neither we nor they can afford to be panicky. Let's start by getting Axe, Mike and Ron over here and talk this through with them, like, now, in the next few minutes, okay?"

"You're the professor, here, Rick, but it is *my* family and I agree we have to sort this all out lickity-split." She rubs her forehead briskly, "Let's *us* go to *them*! Okay?"

"Absolutely, Babe! Let's hold off taking showers for a few minutes, and hop over to see Axe and the other two to see what they suggest, and determine how best to handle the need to protect your family. Then we'll take it from there. Yes?"

She nods agreement. They head out their door, quickly cross the driveway and knock. Axe responds immediately. "Okay," he says, after hearing the first sentence or two. "Come on in. Let's get the boys over here for a quick meeting. He calls them on his two-way, and they appear in less than a minute. "We need to take some immediate action, guys! Here's the whole story." Axe turns to Maddigan, who looks concerned, glances at JP, then explains the call. Maddigan repeats everything he just reported to JP.

Chapter 28

Back to JP's Family and Rick's Jeep

JP follows up on the meeting she and the Professor had with their three police guards, by calling her father with the recommendation that the officers suggested. She gets Pete on the phone and explains a sample of what's been happening:

. . . Damages to the Jeep. . . the middle-of-the-night call that Rick picked up. . . the meeting with Lieutenant Axe, and officers Mike and Ron. . . a much-abbreviated version of being pursued in Costa Rica as reason for their boat trip to the Puerto Plata resort in the Dominican Republic before returning home.

Her father, Pete, a big, strong industrial arts teacher at Seaport County Vocational Tech School, as always, trusted JP's judgment about people and places.

"Well, okay. Timing's good!" he said in response to JP's input. "I was thinking about taking your Mom and sisters up to our New Hampshire lakefront retreat anyway, for a week or so 'til the semester starts for me and both of you guys. You and Rick are certainly welcome to join us to get yourselves—and of course your Mom and sisters—out from under all the hubbub, Y'know?"

JP respectfully declined the offer, but left it open she might change her mind and agreed that was a great idea for the family to go visit the lakefront.

"Mom's school library doesn't open yet either, right? Oh, and when you alert your neighbors to keep an eye on the house, as you always do, be sure to also give them Rick's Jeep CB Radio Handle—The Professor 38521—just in case any issues arise. He should have the Jeep back by tomorrow."

He further agreed and said they'd be leaving tomorrow after an early breakfast, and the only side trip would be a parkway bathroom stop and to pick up some food on the way since clothes and everything else they need is already at the lakefront address.

JP closed the discussion with, "Thanks Dad. I'll be sure to keep you fully informed going forward. I love you so much. Thanks for being so understanding and responsive." Then, she added as a closing thought, "Uh, by the way, Dad, this New Hampshire trip could be even more special for Pam and Olee if you happened to stop at that next mountain farm we went to for veggies that time?" She took a deep breath, then smiled at the thought of what she was about to say. "To visit with that farmer and his wife, y'know—the Golden Retriever breeders, Barrie and Proctor Bonacci? Maybe they've got that puppy the girls have always wanted? One that's like two or three months old, uh, and house trained? I mean, you could tell Mom it's just an added security deal and if it doesn't work out, you can return it on your way back home. Y'think? Maybe Mom could even name it?"

They both laughed and agreed it might be just the right time to do as JP suggests.

"And, she added, "Since my sisters both mentioned that Goldens are their favorite breed when one popped on the TV screen for a minute while Rick and I were there, it might be both a fun responsibility for them to share, and a good diversion. Maybe even an extra layer of protection; and they could even name it," she added with a smile.

ॐঙ

"Hi, is this Proctor Bonacci?"

"Yup! That's me! . . . Who's callin?"

"Hey Proctor! This is Pete Haley the big-shop-teacher-guy you called me when my family and I visited you and your wife Barrie awhile ago? We're on the next mountain, just east of you on the lake?"

"Pete the big-shop-teacher-guy! Right! I remember you. You came lookin' to Barrie's and my farm for veggies. Nice family!"

"Yup, that's me, Proctor. Thanks! Listen, about those great Goldens you breed? You maybe got one a few months old we could stop by to see on the way up to our lakefront place?"

"Absolutely!" Bonacci responded. "In fact, we got two brothers right now—a couple a hundred each or both for three—they're two months old and bright as all get-out. The next day or two? If I know you're coming, I'll be sure to let Liz know to hold 'em for you."

"Great! Probably get there mid-to-late afternoon tomorrow. See you then."

ॐঙ

"Y'know, Joan, the girls mentioned and I've been thinkin' it might be a good idea to stop on our way to the lake at that farm we've been to on the next mountain and load up with fresh veggies, y'think?"

"Great idea, Pete! Let's do it!"

JP's sisters, near hysterical from over-hearing JP's call, cover their mouths as their father confirmed their expectations by suggesting a farm visit to their Mom en route to the lakefront. Mom was of course totally unaware of the dog deal as she waited for them in the driveway while they locked up the house.

136

೭∞೭

"Well, we need to keep you guys cookin' and give you a chance for happy lives," Axe said, standing between them. Then quietly mumbled to himself: "Wish I was a preacher and not a retired cop," as he put one hand on each of their shoulders. All three smiled.

JP, Maddigan, and Axe stood admiring the repaired Jeep's brand-new tires, double-insulated canvas roof, with back and side windows, new seat covers, and a full gas tank/oil change, wash 'n' wax job. Even a replaced dented old fender.

"Yup," Axe said, "and Ron's returning your rental car. The Jeep and rental have both been paid for with County Police Funds!"

"WOW!" they said in unison with ear-to-ear grins.

"Well, we're both glad you're back on active duty, instead of being that preacher you wished you were," Maddigan said. "And we wish we could find the right words to tell you how grateful we are for all of this."

JP interrupted Maddigan's pause with a wink. "In case you didn't figure it out yet, Rick can only find the right words in front of a class or me. Really, Axe, you, Ron and Mike just took away a pile of stress that lets us be 100% focused on doing what it takes to get this sick-mobster-mentality stuff out of our lives. Thank you!"

Before Axe could even respond, Maddigan turned to face Axe and added, "How about a quick ride in this new Jeep up onto the beach Four Wheel Drive Trail and back?"

"Thanks, you two. I'll take a raincheck on that beach Jeep Trail offer. Right now, I'm starting a next-step meeting with Mike and Ron. Fill ya both in later."

They nod.

೭∞೭

"Well, Professor, that was a great quick-trip test for the old new Jeep," JP summed up the twenty-minute ride up to the beach and through some sand dunes and back.

"Yup" he replied with a smile. "They did one hell of a job. It even drives better than when it was new!" He smiles. "Being in such good shape with a full gas tank," he pulls into their driveway and parks, "I'm thinkin' maybe it'd be a good idea after all to take up your Dad's invite to join them—at least for a couple a days—in New Hampshire."

JP's green eyes near explode with bright light as she disconnects her seatbelt.

"I'd love to see the place again," he continues. "I mean we haven't been there in what? Almost two years? I'd love to see all the additions he made to the house, and the anchored dock he added to the lake, plus it's no secret that I love your Mom's cookin!"

She climbs into his lap, her back to the steering wheel, gives him a big hug and kiss. They both laugh, slowly untangle and climb out of the Jeep.

"We need to tell Axe first."

Chapter 29

CA stutters & Spits—NJ Wheels & Deals

"Okay, Gentlemen," says Warden Tantrumatto, arms folded. "Now that we've exchanged niceties, I need to ask you the real reason you're here, since I checked both of you out and you're not the amateurs your Chief would have me believe."

"Fair enough, Warden," Detective Infusino replied. "Cutting to the chase, as you suggest, makes a big difference in the three of us not having to waste each other's time. So, in the interests of time, I'm gonna ask my detective partner here, Detective Focazio, to be very blunt about this and explain why we're here. Ron?"

Focazio takes over. "Here's the bottom line, Warden: We're here to find out what your relationship is with Solamenté beyond that he's a Solitary Confinement Prisoner of yours, because we learned recently that he has been managing to communicate with Mafioso gangsters in our State for more than a year when—as you know—he's not to have any communication with anyone beyond his cell and a handful of Guards."

Before the Warden can respond, Infusino adds, "We know he's been granted some kind of leniency here in violation of his verdict and your internal prisoner management system. So, before we complete and file our report to New Jersey and California Prison System Management—and both Governors—we're here to give you a last chance to avoid legal charges and find out what your take is on this investigation. *Now!*"

"L-listen, d-d-de-t-t-tectives, I-I-I don't know wha-whatcha your talkin' a-about, a-a-and, I think you b-both better g-get outta my office b-before I—"

Infusino cuts him off. "Cut the BS, Warden! You're in this up to your neck, and I'll tell you that if you want to stay in your Warden position longer than tomorrow, with both State and Federal Government orders ending your career that are already drawn up and ready to be released, you're gonna have to work with us, not against us, to settle this mess. Do you understand what we're saying? Do you understand that you will be tried for aiding and abetting a solitary confinement convicted murderer who has been threatening highly-respected citizens?"

The Warden, visibly shaken, starts to jitter and stutter. "B-b-but, I don't c-control all this s-stuff you're referring to; I only h-hear about it from the g-guards, and I've t-t-tried to p-p-put limits on h-him, b-b-but—"

Focazio cuts him off... "Cut the crap, Warden! Your Guards know what's going on! And we know Solamenté controls the information channels. You think your Guards are not gonna talk if they're put on the stand with their jobs and their family lives on the line?"

Tantrumatto's now stuttering fulltime: "B-b-but . . ."

"Listen, Warden, we are not here to get you fired" says Infusino, sounding almost apologetic. "We are here to shut down all communication channels between Solamenté and Mafia people in our State. We are asking you to step in and change whatever has been going on to *nothing* is going on! *And,* if you can't make that happen immediately, we think the Governors of your State and our State *can* and *will* make it happen. And, yes, that's likely to cost you, Tony—along with some of your guards—your jobs!" He pauses to let that sink in, then adds, "And in all likelihood, that will mean zero benefits as well!"

"W-wait a minute, y-you guys. I c-can't afford to lose th-this j-job, I—my fa-family..."

"Look, Warden," Focazio picks up on Tantrumatto's nervousness, "Here's the bottom line. We need to know right here, right now, that you're going to work with us and not share even one single drop of information we're discussing here with Solamenté or any of the Guards, or literally—with *anyone,* even family if you want to keep this job longer than twenty-four hours! In other words, you offer *no* explanations of any kind to *anyone*—including your family, friends, prisoners, other prison workers, media people, politicians—even your minister! Got it? Bottom line is that one—just *one* slip-up will cost you and your family dearly. Soooo?"

"B-but what h-happens if—"

Infusino cuts him off. "There are no if's, Warden," he responds. "It's simple. You just shut it down! 100%! Stop all communication between you and your guards with this brain-sick-solitary-confined prisoner, and his spokesmen. Solamenté's confinement was a deliberate judicial decision—keep him in solitary, which means twenty-four-seven under all circumstances. No exceptions! Y'got it?"

"Y-y-yes. I understand. I-I promise that I will c-cut him off from all c-contacts starting immediately." A long pause. He shakes his head as if trying to wake up and quickly tries to shift gears. "C-can I offer you b-boys some c-coffee or sometin?"

"No thanks," says Infusino, as he and his partner stand. "Just keep your promise. We will keep tabs on you and check back with you on a daily basis until we're sure this has resolved itself. How's ten in the morning your time for those calls?"

The Warden nods approval.

141

"And," adds Focazio, "You call us—ten in the morning every day! Got it?" He hands the Warden both of their NJ State Police business cards. "If *anything* changes from what we have agreed to here—*anything*—you call us immediately!"

The Warden nods affirmatively.

"One last thought," Infusino adds. "If you fail in any way to be 100% in on this agreement—like, for example, and this is just an example, not calling us promptly at ten every day?—within minutes of missing that deadline, you can be sure I'll be on the phone with my old high-school *and* Coast Guard *buddy,* John Armstrong, your new Governor of California. I hear-tell that he has a little pull with your bosses! Got it?"

Tantrumatto nods. "Let m-me g-get someone t-to show y-you out!" he says, clearly shaken by the thought of Governor John Armstrong getting involved.

"No need for any escort here, Warden. We got this place figured out. Just call the Guard out front to open and close the gate. We'll talk with you when you call at ten your time tomorrow morning. Anyway," Infusino smiles, "You have a nice week!"

They all shake hands. The detectives take a quick look over their shoulders as they leave Tantrumatto's office and see the Warden visibly shaken, face down in his hands, on his desktop, the same desktop he's no doubt usually pounding. Two guards show them to the main entrance and through the double gates, which close behind them.

They walk casually to their rental car.

"So, Whaddaya think, Ron? Ya think He got it?"

"Yup!" Focazio responds, "I think he got more than the message, and more than he bargained for. And *you* are a great partner! You said all the right things in the right way at the right time! The only tantrum that Tantrumatto can have now will be with himself! I'm just not sure how convinced he'll feel about actually making the commitment to immediately and completely disconnect from Solamenté. It's gonna come down to whether he elects to follow our demands or reports all of this to the bad guys. And, of course if he does that, we have no choice except to blow this whole thing wide open, which as you know, means we'd have to be prepared to deal with national news media, and all kinds of internal police politics. Y'know what I mean, Mike?"

"Well, you're right, Ron. And that would create a whole new set of problems for JP and the Professor, y'know? There's no doubt his choices will dictate responses from both sides of the issue. The thing is we have innocent, valuable, positive-impact lives in the balance here with JP and Maddigan. The ultimatum we spelled out for this Tantrum guy may come back and smack us in the face." Mike takes a deep breath, then continues. "He could also be muscled into doing everything we told him not to do. I mean we literally opened a can of worms here. Somehow, we gotta figure out how to make this work, beyond his words. He may be ducking the issue just to get us outta town, y'know? Mike turns to his partner. "How 'bout some lunch and a beer on our way back?"

They both smile.

"Great suggestion!" Ron says, as he pats Mike's shoulder.

Chapter 30

Surprise Visits—NH, CA & NJ

"Y'know, JP, we visited a lot of places these past few months, but none like New Hampshire. I'm glad we sidetracked to come up here with your family. On top of that, how much fun was it to stop off at that farm and fit these two great puppies into the Jeep for the last hour drive to your folk's lakefront escape? I think your Mom was surprised, but she seemed to relate to the pups as well as your sisters and Pete. Whaddaya think?"

"I agree about the puppies and love having them with us in the Jeep right now. Of course, they look a bit scared at the moment, but wait 'til they jump in the lake and learn to swim to Dad's new dock! And, yeah, Mom's gonna love having them around. She'll probably take charge, y'know? She'll feed and walk them with Pam and Olee."

"I was thinkin' the same thing, Green Eyes. Pam and Olee were jumpin' outta their skin when your Mom agreed to the deal and your Dad put the cash up for both pups! Did you ever have a dog before?"

She grinned and nodded, "Sure. When I was little."

Rick returns the grin. "You were little?"

Her one eye shut fake frown, and snarly response came fast. "Actually, yes! I was little when I had a sleepy old beagle, Morris, who had a hard time keeping his belly off the floor, but I played with him anyway. He was pretty good at Peek-A-Boo!" She laughed.

It almost seemed like the two Goldens understood the verbal exchange in the front seats as they began to act restless in their back-seat strapped-down cage.

"Hey, you two!" JP said as she turned, then laughed at seeing one on top of the other. She undid her seatbelt as Rick pulled to the side of the road, then reached back into the cage to separate the pups and make sure all was well. JP strapped herself back into her seat.

"Are they okay?" Maddigan asked. JP grinned and nodded.

Twenty minutes later, they were on the thirty-degree uphill dirt road that ran along side, but was a hundred feet above the lake level. Her family had arrived a few minutes ahead of them and were unloading luggage and farm-fresh veggies, along with an assortment of carpentry tools Pete secretly stowed away to build a double-sized doghouse.

The girls ran to the Jeep as it pulled into the driveway and both of them practically climbed into the puppies' cage the minute Rick pulled up the parking brake. Lots of skirmishing, giggling, petting, running, hugging and barking topped off their arrival.

⌘

Officer Focazio says to partner Officer Infusino, "Y'know, Mike, we've visited a lot of places over the years, but nothin' outta State, except Manhattan and Philadelphia, and—for sure—nothin' about a questionable Warden all the way across the country! Whaddaya think we're headed into? How do you figure this? Y'think this is like MenzaMenz stuff, Mike, or are we headed for some deep-shit stress here?"

"Uh, deep MenzaMenz shit, would be my best guess," Mike answers with a big grin. "But," he adds, "that's why we both became cops in the first place to help good people dig outta deep shit! Truth is, Ron; that your guess is as good as mine, I imagine it's a big pile of stress, and no pill's gonna make it go away. I think we need a couple or three action plans to be able to cover all the bases—our Italiano asses if things get edgy. I figure we gotta just take it as it comes and be sure we stay on top."

Focazio nods agreement. "Both the Chief and the college," he says, "are counting on us, and of course this JP and professor couple. They seem like good people, y'know?"

"Yup! I agree with you about them, Amico!" Focazio laughs, then says, "I agree with your takin'-it-as-it-comes strategy and makin' sure we stay on top! It's like a wrestling match, right?" He gives Mike a playful punch on the arm.

"And it's a damn good thing we're both in A-1 shape just in case, y'know?" Mike answers with a smile and thumb's up!

"Gentlemen!" says the airline desk attendant to the two officers, "your flight will be boarding shortly. Can we get you both seated ahead of that? We're not too crowded tonight, so wherever you choose will be fine. We'll be opening the gate for the other passengers in three or four minutes. They both thanked the attendant and headed down the boarding ramp. They chose adjacent aisle seats in the first row behind First Class.

The two detectives sit calm-before-the-storm relaxed, as other passengers—most look like businesspeople. Not much family travel at this hour—begin to board, stuff the overhead racks, and settle into their seats. The almost six-hour non-stop flight is expected to land early enough to avoid rush-hour traffic. They agree to work out a three-way Action Plan for the prison visit.

As passengers entered and settled, the two spoke quietly about their objectives needing to be specific, flexible, and realistic in order to complete their "OST"—Objectives, Strategies, and Tactics—approach, and that whatever they came up with would be dictated by any of three possible Warden Attitude scenarios—Receptivity; Antago-nism, or Laissé Faire—which would guide their decision-making.

Then they slept, oblivious to quiet nearby chatter, food wrap-per-rattling, beverage ice clinking and pilot or crew announcements.

ॐॐ

Chief Oleson had the California State Police Chief set the ten o'clock meeting with the Warden as a request to provide some help and prison management expertise to two New Jersey cops who would be visiting to learn some big prison politics and management processes, and will appreciate some private time in the morning with the Warden. He realized he risked losing the CASP Chief's trust if things go awry.

ॐॐ

Axe opened his Laraine Avenue front door to find Chief John Oleson standing there, visually scanning the empty sandy streets, side-walks and driveways and the edge of the slight street incline to the sum-mer beach hidden behind a row of oceanfront dunes.

"Hey! JohnO! C'mon in! Waz up?"

"Well, this time," Oleson said reaching into his coat, "I brought you coffee and a Mrs. Obco donut!" He stepped in. Axe closed the door. "Just one donut?" Axe asked and laughed. "Where'd you park, by the way, up at the beach by the fishermen?"

"Good guess, Axe. Didn't want to disrupt your spy operations on this street!" Axe chuckled. "Yeah, and it ain't even summertime yet! Ya hear from our boys yet?"

"No, but not to worry. I know you know, but they're the two best we got here, and if anybody can infiltrate that either evil or dumb-ass Warden's barricade, they can. In fact, I think they'll turn this whole mess upside-down in no time, which would be great for all of us."

Oleson scans the little cottage and steps to look out the front window. Sensing the Chief had more to say, Axe sips his surprise coffee and bites his donut.

"I'd like our two guys to work it out of course," Chief Oleson continues, "so I've made every resource possible available. As you know, I have lots of confidence in what they are capable of. But, just in case they run into trouble, I'm hold'n out my one last option—my old high school buddy who I'd prefer not to cash in chips with, but will if need be. He's now the new Governor of California, John Armstrong. He oversees the State prison system with considerable input to Federal prison operations in that State."

"Sounds like a plan, JohnO. Please keep me posted."

Oleson looks out the window, and continues. "Let's review some options on dealing with our local Mafia friends. We will, as you know, have to live with them long after this mess is cleaned up!"

"Because they're the guys who bring the money into town that pays our salaries."

"Yup! But that doesn't mean we shouldn't call their hand when we need to!"

Just as Oleson steps toward the door, Axe's phone rings. They look at one another as Axe picks up the receiver. "Yes, just a minute!" He reaches to hand the phone to Oleson. "This one's for you, Chief!"

Oleson listens intently, squints his eyes, then grins.

"Okay, thanks for the call. Good job. Catch you in the AM," he says and hangs up. "Well," he turns to Axe, "sounds like the boys did their job. Now we have to wait to see if we get the results we want. Should know by tomorrow morning. We'll keep you posted. Be sure to let me know if anything comes up. Oh, and, there's two more Mrs. Obco's donuts for you in the bag here by the door!" He smiles as he steps to open both the bag and the door.

"Wow! Thanks, Boss. Catch you later!"

Just as the Chief steps out the door, he notices out the corner of his eye, a foot climbing into JP and the professor's kitchen window. He quickly turns back into Axe's living room and puts a *quiet* finger to his lips as he unholsters his ankle gun.

Axe puts the donut bag down as he also unholsters and motions to the Chief to follow him to his back door, which directly faces Maddigan and JP's cottage. They exit without making a sound to stand in the shadows next to the window the foot went through. Oleson gestures Axe to get behind him in the shadow against the wall.

They wait and glance at one another with understanding. They hear thumps and bumps inside. Just as Oleson ducks under the window and moves to the far side, Axe steps quickly into Oleson's spot, and a male head sticks out to find two guns in his face. The culprit climbs out with an open hand raised, then both hands up as he hits the ground.

"Please, don't shoot! Please! This wasn't my idea. Please don't shoot! I can't—"

"Shut up! Get face down in the sand. Hands behind your back!" Commands Oleson. With one knee on the invader's back, Axe cuffs both wrists and ankles while the Chief reads the twenty-something man his rights. Then Axe tells him to roll over and sit. With both guns pointed, they look him in the eye. Axe asks him his name and where he's from.

"Newark," he answers, then adds "but I am only here because my boss told me to get into this cabin and see what I could find in the way of any past or planned paperwork for travel for some guy named Maddigan and his girlfriend, JP—but I couldn't find anything like that. Just some clothes and some cash. I left the clothes alone. The cash, he whines, is in my pocket. Axe reaches and pulls out ten $500 bills!

"This?" he asks, staring the suspect in the eye.

"Yeah," the culprit mumbles.

"Your name?" Axe asks. "Joe DiPasqualini," he mumbles.

"Okay, Mr. DiPasqualini, well, we're gonna take you in on breaking and entering and grand larceny charges. You have a lawyer?" DiPasqualini shakes his head. "Then just sit right there! If you move more than two inches, we shoot, you understand?" DiPasqualini nods.

Chapter 31

Stirring Solamente's Pudding?

"Y'know, the kid we caught climbing out the cottage window could possibly be that three-AM caller who the Professor reported. We should arrange to question him about that. If he was the caller, then my next guess is that he's one of the New Jersey Mob's sons-in-training, and that could be a good thing! You know what I mean? It could give us something to bargain with for ending Solamenté's control, y'think?" Seaport County Police Chief reasoned with Axe as they sipped coffee at the College Diner.

"Makes sense to me, Chief," Axe responds, "except I'd hate to see that kid back out on the street anytime soon. Breaking and entering, grand theft, and carrying with no license, plus who knows what else? How about we arrange to question him as soon as we get some details on who he is, where he's from, and all that other good stuff that our jailers ask new prisoners about?"

"Sounds like a plan, Axe. I'll get a time set ASAP to poke for more info. We don't want anyone posting bail for him before we can get some answers from him. Can we delay that?"

"I think it can be arranged. We can delay the earliest bail-post time—if there is any—I'm not so sure bail will even be allowed once the judge sees the amount of money involved, a gun with no license, and sees my note about the kid's connections."

❧

"I'm tellin' ya, Warden," Guard "Figgy" Newton knuckle-raps the Warden's desktop, "I got a family to feed, and I ain't lookin' to stir things up any more than they already are. Maybe you can bully your way through this cause your position's got more clout than us Guards have, but I gotta be honest 'bout Solamenté's existence here if my job's on the line. I never thought much about all his BS or his little lunch-time gatherings in the Courtyard, or 'bout doin' him little favors like deliverin' a note to you or to another inmate, ya know whadda mean? Just parta the job, y'know? But from what you're sayin' there's some top people in government lookin' ta shut him up and some top people in the Mafia lookin' ta mak'im a hero. All I want is ta do my job, and support my family. Y'unnerstand?"

Before Tantrumatto can even respond, three of the other Guards who work with Newton step forward to express their agreement with him about the risk of losing their jobs and benefits. One guard with a family of five has two years left 'til retirement on twenty years' worth of benefits and savings The other has four years to go with sixteen years in and a family of six to support.

"Where the hell we gonna go if this job falls through?" says one of them?

"Yeah," says the third one, "and it's even more than the money. What the hell else can we be expected to know how to do except be guards at this point? I mean I'm sixty-three years old!! And whadda our families do in the meantime?"

❧

151

JP and Rick are upstairs chatting with JP's Mom, Joan, about all that JP's Dad has done over the past two years' worth of escape weekends to strengthen, secure and beautify the family's lakefront vacation home in the mountains getaway, but most of their real-time attention has been on the two puppies and the mesmerizing mountain views sweeping through the living room picture window.

JP's Dad and her two sisters are downstairs, staring out the heavy-duty glass slider doors to the footpath and steps down to the waterfront, to the new anchored floating dock sixty feet off the shore . and backdropped by the mountains across the lake.

The oldest of JP's two younger sisters, Pamela, walks over to sit on the armrest of the lounge chair her Father occupies with his youngest daughter, Olie, on his lap.

Pamela pats his arm and quietly asks, "Hey Dad! What would you and Mom say if we name one of the two puppies Flokie 'cause we both like that name and then name the other one Bollen to match up with my sister 'Olie' so together with her name, it spells Oliebollen— that famous Dutch donut you and Mom always serve and talk about on New Year's Eve?" The long, teenage-style question promptly followed in a clearly rehearsed presentation from JP's youngest sister, looking hopefully up at the both of them.

"Pamela and I both voted already, but we'd like to know what you and Mom think."

Pete laughs.: "I think those are great names, but you'll have to get your Mom's vote and of course JP's and Rick's too!"

"You, Dad, are Sooper Dooper! Thanks," says Olie, as she scrambles off his lap and grabs Pamela's arm.

"Yeah, we were just gonna run upstairs and ask her," says Pamela "and of course JP and Rick too, what they all think."

Then without even taking a breath, Pamela and Olie raced right into Part II of their spiel with Pete.

"By the way, Dad, what would you think if we give Flokie to JP and Rick?" she asked with a big ear-to-ear grin, outdone only by her little sister Olie's ear-to-ear grin. "And, that way, Olie and I would keep Bollen? And when we all get together, the two brothers can too, y'think?"

"Yup, I agree with my sister, Dad. In fact, we voted two to zero on that!"

Their message was simply that they had thought of everything and were seeking support for their decision. The three of them smiled at each other, then the two girls ran up the stairs to repeat their sales pitch. Pete was left laughing to himself while quietly predicting their success. Five minutes later, the happy shouts, barks and upstairs foot stomps said it all. Pete headed up to be part of the celebration.

❧

Apple paces back and forth in front of them, slapping his hands, offset by a quiet breathy whisper. "Sompin's not right. Sompin's goin' on. My messages don't seem to be getting' through."

Solamenté wrings his hands, spits at their feet. He punches his right fist into his left hand with a slap that seemed to echo off all the Courtyard walls. Heads turned—guards and prisoners both —rom as much as thirty feet away.

After a couple of minutes of quiet stares, glances, and Solamenté's name whispered in other sections of the courtyard, he follows with a harsh, angry but much quieter whisper.

"Did one of-you screw-ups say or write sumtin'? Are we still workin' together here or what?"

Bo Strangles, Chop Sooey, and Phil Thee look at each other. They all appear to be puzzled.

"Waddayamean?" Bo asks him, Chop and Phil nod in agreement with Bo's question.

"What I mean," came the harshest whispered response yet, accompanied by a wad of flying green phlegm spit over his left shoulder

153

in the general direction of Thee and Sooey,"is that somebody's closin' down the communications channel here. I passed a note for the Warden to the Guard last night and got no answer. Zip! Nada! Sompin's screwed-up. Any ideas?"

He scans the three grubby faces. They all look at one another and no one speaks.

"Well," says Solamenté, "keep your eyes and ears open." The Courtyard Horn blasts. They all stand.

"Catchya tomorrow," he mumbles.

They head for the tunnel back to their cells under strict Guard control on both sides.

❧❧

"I can't believe we now own a dog, Rick! I mean we're not even married and we own a dog?"

JP's hands are on top of her head with fingers locked as she watches Maddigan stroke Flokie with the grooming brush JP's Mom bought for them while they were in New Hampshire. He laughs at her comment and hands-on-head pose.

"Y'know, JP, Flokie really is a beautiful dog. Uh, not as beautiful as you, of course, but he's gonna make a great addition to our deck and our Anchor Out's when we get another boat after all this stuff is over. And I love seeing you with your hands on your head because when I can see them, I know your hands can't be getting us into any trouble." He grins.

"Well, Mr. Boat Captain-Professor, y'know what they say about All Hands On Deck and I know you know about playing with a full deck, and—"

He responds mimicking a tough guy. "Yeah, an' I donnwanna hafta deck ya!" Then he kisses her.

Chapter 32

It's Time to Check the Facts!

"Hey, Axe, this is Rick Maddigan. How's it going?

"Hi. Professor! All's good here. How are you? How's JP? How's New Hampshire?

"Great! Great! and Great! And, we have a new family member. His name is Flokie! Flokie's a couple-of-month's old male Golden Retriever! He's from JP's Family who bought him and his brother Bollen. JP and I are keeping Flokie, hoping for some added protection going forward. Of course, he'll need some training, y'know, but how's everything there?"

"All's well here. No hassles. Flokie, huh? How did that happen? The name, I mean. The only Flokie I ever knew was a sheep dog who had total control of his own flock."

"Yeah, well, so does this Flokie! Him and his brother, Bollen, who JP's little sisters are keeping, have control of JP's whole family, and even me!" Maddigan chuckles.: "So, anyway, what's going on, Axe? Any news or progress?"

Axe responds with a report of the attempted break-in and reassures him about the recovered cash as he fills Maddigan in on and what he and Chief Oleson have been planning. He then confides in Maddigan with an update of the two detectives' overnight mission to Solamenté's prison warden, and the plans to involve Axe's FBI Agent friend.

"Based on all we know so far, I think you're in the right place at the right time for this week, and you can rest assured we are keeping an eye on your property—and, of course, JP's family's home—twenty-four-seven. I will call you there immediately if anything changes."

"Thank you, Axe. I can't begin to tell you how grateful JP and I and her family are of your time, attention and diligence. If it weren't for you and your team, none of us would be able to even sleep at night, y'know? We are truly grateful for your leadership."

"Yeah, well, you're more than welcome Rick. We just hate to see people like you and JP, who are true heroes, have to bank on the police in order to rest assured that it's safe enough to travel to New Hampshire for a family weekend, instead of sitting home nerve-wracked over the possibility that a solitary-confinement prisoner in California could intrude on your lives by commandeering evil forces here in New Jersey to not accept your heroism. You just relax and have fun up there. We'll see you next week!"

"Thanks, Axe. It's the first time all year JP and I have felt mentally relaxed, and that's only because of you and your men. I definitely need to buy you and your team a couple of beers when we get back! Maybe I'll even get you a Mrs. Obco donut, which I hear is your favorite!" Axe laughs. Both smile as they hang up.

～◦⊱

"What did he say?" she asks Maddigan.

"Well, JP, he told me all's well, that there was an attempted break-in, but they caught the guy and nothing's been damaged or taken, that things have quieted down, that our cottage and your family's home are both safe, that they are working twemty-four-hour shifts on alert, that the Chief is figuring out a 'Master Plan' for controlling New Jersey Mafia guys, and that the word is out that this Solamenté creep is getting his comeuppance from the two cops we met—Focazio and Infusino— and that it will probably all end with a total shut-down on California's number one solitary confinement prisoner who has been anything but solitary, or confined."

"Whew! Well, that's a relief, at least for the moment," JP responds, "and hopefully it's forever, y'think?"

"Hopefully is right, JP! Y'know how great it will be to get us both back onto a boat deck, running our Anchor-Out sessions?"

"You ain't just kiddin' Professor!" They hug, then kiss: "Mum-mpf!"

᚜᚛

"You got that right, Guard! You tell that asshole warden I ain't got no patience about restoring any open communication channel, and that I want to connect personally and directly tonight with my Jersey contacts, and I want no fookin' delay or interruption comin' from his office. You tellum that! Just like I said it."

He takes a deep breath. "And tellum if he don't get his act together and support my open phone channel needs, I will get the word out to all California and New Jersey newspapers about him proving once again that he's on the wrong side of law enforcement by shuttin' down my calls and I will personally see to it that he and his family suffer *forever* for him takin' the high road here. Got it?"

"Y-y-y-yeah!, I got it. Calm down there, Mr. Solamenté. I'm sure he'll get this straightened out like yer askin!"

"I ain't askin' you, doofbag! I'm tellin' you!" He pauses and spits to the floor through his cell-wall food opening, almost hitting Guard Figgy Newton's feet. Newton shuts the opening and hustles off down the hall to the Warden's office.

❧❦

"Sorry to barge in on you, Warden and—" He looks to the suit-and-tie-stranger sitting next to Warden Tantrumatto's desk. "—and I hope I'm not interrupting, but—" The Warden squints at Newton.

"Well, we do usually knock first, Figgy! What's up?"

"Uh, sorry, but you-know-who's bitchin' 'bout shuttin' down his phone channel and he's threatening you with some newspaper contacts. He—"

"Not now, N-Newton; this is F-F-FBI Agent R-Randy R-R-Robbins here."

Robbins nods at the Guard.

"And we're in the m-middle of a meeting. Sooo m-move along and d-don't worry about any threats. It's p-part of the job. Later!"

Newton looks stunned by the Warden's stuttering refusal to hear him out. He quickly leaves and closes the door.

"S-Sorry for the interruption, Agent R-Robbins. Now, as I was saying, the fact is that one of the th-things we do here that you may not see in N-New J-Jersey, is that we grant periodic phone calls to and from what I would c-call B-Best Behavior inmates."

The Warden stands and walks toward his second-floor window on the courtyard. He scans the second-floor Guards' walkway while talking over his shoulder to Agent Robbins.

"We do this," he continues, "because we've learned the h-hard way that shutting them d-down 100% simply creates ill feelings and encourages b-bad behavior, which, in some cases actually c-costs us in excess of existing medical insurance c-coverage. In other cases, we've had a n-number of prisoners and on r-rare occasion, g-guards, suffer physical issues, like b-broken teeth and bones, an occasional c-concussion, you know what I m-mean? So, yes, we reward g-good behavior when it's appropriate."

"And when might that have been appropriate for Solitary Confinement prisoners like Solamenté, Chop Sooey, Bo Strangles and Phil

Thee?" Robbins asks, talking to the back of the Warden's head. "We understand these four are being catered to, and given telephone and other privileges not offered to other prisoners. Why?"

"Th-the f-facts are t-that." He stops and shakes his head.

Without answering, the Warden excuses himself while walking toward and through his open door, leaving Agent Robbins sitting opposite the Warden's vacated desk and window. Robbins stands, glances out the window to the Courtyard below at Guards pacing the walkway.

A few minutes pass. The Guard who had escorted Robbins to the office arrives. He asks if he can accompany Robbins to the exit, explaining that the Warden had left an apology message for having to leave the premises so promptly, but he had to attend an important meeting. Robbins nods with a smirk and follows the Guard to the exit.

Chapter 33

A Week of Worry and Joyful Loss

"Y'know, Rick, I'm so glad we made that trip to New Hampshire to spend time with my parents and sisters and got the dogs and to have ended-up being able to keep Flokie." She smiles as she glances toward their new Golden Retriever asleep under the kitchen table. "And for the girls and my folks to keep Bollen, and the Jeep to be like new again, and Axe and his officers, Mike and Ron, and Chief Oleson, and—"

"Whoa there, young lady!" Maddigan interrupts, "Ya' think today's Thanksgiving or something? Save me the tail and some stuffing. I mean where're you headed with all this thankfulness? And, by the way, I didn't hear my name in there," as he postures with his chin in and hands on hips with one foot forward.

"Well, first of all, Rick, you look like a dork!" He lowers his chin, pulls his foot back and puts his hands in his pockets. "Thank you! Second:, I know you're as happy about Bollen and your revitalized Jeep as I am. And I know we're equally thankful for the help and support of Axe's police team. Plus, last time I checked, you and I were deeply in love. So, what's with all this insecurity?"

Maddigan responds by stepping toward her, toe-to-toe, leaning down to hug and kiss her, then whispering in her ear, "You know I love you heart and soul, even more than my Jeep or your family, the police team, and Bollen and Flokie combined." He takes a deep breath. "Of course I'm just as thankful as you are too, but I *am* still worried about us being chased halfway around the world by such a sick array of gangsters who are being commandeered by that sicko Solamenté creep from his so-called Solitary Confinement Cell on the other side of the United States."

Maddigan pauses, lowers his head and takes yet another deep breath. JP remains silent and doesn't interrupt his flow of consciousness.

"All of this prompts me to worry about you! About your family! About us! Like what happens if the police can't control this mess or these evil threats?" He gently reaches to touch her cheek. "Do we need to live in some kind of solitary confinement cell of our own? Sorry, Babe! It's just that no one in the world has ever made me happier than you, and I don't ever want to risk losing that love you send my way day after day!"

܀

"Your way, day after day? I didn't realize you were a poet also, you big schlunk! P.S. I love you too!" She blinks her eyes innocently at him. "So when are you ever going to ask me to marry you? And will it be a my way-day after day kinda rhyme?" Both smile.

After pausing for a long-deep-breath-moment, he says, "I want to, JP. I promise to ask you soon, but let's get through this mess we're in first, okay?"

"Yes! Thank you! But I love you too much to wait like forever!"

He nods agreement and mutters to himself, "Me too!"

She seals her dozen words with a big one-minute kiss!

❧✦❧

"Hey, Randy Robbins! How are you? I heard you were an FBI Agent, but working in the Bureau's Lab rarely has much crossover to you field-agent guys," says FBI Lab Specialist, Sara Cranston. They exchange hugs, back pats and handshakes.

"Yeah, I'm good, thanks Sara! They call me Red these days, by the way. Anyway, great to be on the same team again!" Robbins says. "Waddaja find out about this Pasquale kid?"

"Well, Red, the lab reports show the Pasquale kid—whose actual name is Pasquale Antonio DiPasquale, and who, as you know, Axe and Chief Oleson caught climbing out of JP and Professor Maddigan's cottage window the other day—had a whole lot more than the ten $500 bills and an illegal gun in his pockets." Sara pauses to think. "The lab checked out his jeans and we found his back left pocket had half of a plastic straw in it, and that all four pockets were lined with heavy traces of cocaine. He had to be delivering and snorting it just before they nailed him. And the kid—wait 'til you hear this one!—belongs to Mafia Moneybags:,Mario Antonio DiPasquale who owns half of Newark—uh, not counting some unknown hunk of the airport!"

"Well, that's great work, Sara! Thank you!" Robbins gave her a thumb's up! "I did a little homework too," he says. "Found out the father-on DiPasquale drug-money team is one that Solamenté was working with since long before the big boat bust and murder charges that put him in Solitary in the first place. So, it all adds up to what prompted these goons to put JP Haley and her Professor partner Maddigan in Mafia gun sights to begin with. And you've just confirmed it all. So I'm going to file a request for you to get a Gold Medal!" She laughed.

❧✦❧

"Well," said Special Agent Focazio, smiling at the phone, "congratulations, Warden! You're right on time as requested. What's going on there and what can we do to help?"

"We've sh-sh-shut down all G-G-Guard and Prison communications with S-Solamenté except for any necessary ph-physician visits which will be s-s-strictly controlled and accompanied by t-two of our G-Guards from other cell b-b-blocks. Only bad part is we're s-starting to g-get some heat from the guys h-he spends C-Courtyard t-time with.

"Good work, Warden Tantrumatto! Keep it up—at all costs— keep it up! Don't let his bad-guy associates take charge. *You* are The Boss. Nobody there in Solitary—Guards OR prisoners—should have any say about anything, y'hear?"

The Warden looks down. "G-gotcha!"

Anything we can be helpful with here, let us know. Talk with you tomorrow. Ten your time. Have a good day!"

ॐक

"So, what do you think we should do here, Jim?" asks Seaport County Community College President: Dr. Barry Davidson, as he looks apprehensively at his number one confidant.

"Well," Dean Oliviero replies, "the money from Professor Maddigan and JP Haley is in the bank. And I understand it'll be enough — actually more than enough—to cover all construction and equipment costs."

"Well, that's *great*, Jim!" President Davidson responds, then hesitates. "So, what is the delay all about that you mentioned in the message you left me?"

"Nothing serious, Barry. We just need to meet with Rick and JP to get their final okay to proceed. I'm sure they have some plans they would like to suggest."

"Such as?"

"Well, for example, Maddigan is interested in having his top radio-experienced student run the broadcasting part of the facility, and JP had someone in mind for the newspaper part, and they wanted to meet with each of those two folks first before recommending them."

Davidson nods.

Oliviero continues, "We do have a couple more weeks before construction commitments, and I have calls into both of them; they're on their way back from New Hampshire where they visited with JP's family at their summer home.

"Okay, Jim. Thank you. Just keep me posted, and let me know if you need anything to kickoff this fantastic project! And, thank you for all you do here."

"My pleasure, Barry. I'll keep you posted."

They shake hands with grins on both their faces.

ॐ

Sirens! Whistles! Shouts! Chaos! Gunfire! Armed Guards swarm the Courtyard! Scores of Prisoners are backed up to the walls at gunpoint as the prison medic's small emergency golf cart races to the concrete bench-encircled center of the prison courtyard.

Bo, Chop, and Phil kneel—all with their fingers-locked-hands-behind-their-heads postures, proclaiming innocence—over the bloody, tortured naked-from-the-waist-down body of Solamenté.

Warden Tantrumatto stands at his office window, looking down on the scene in the courtyard. He has a cautious smile on his face. The Guard intercom announced that Solamenté was on his last legs, taking his last breaths—as he reportedly was once before—just before being transported to this prison years ago.

The Warden connects into the Medic's intercom and learns that one of the prison's longest serving sentence prisoners, Phil Thee, actually choked Solamenté by stuffing a torn-out section of his bed sheet down the mobster's throat and into his nose as Chop Sooey and Bo Strangles alternated between holding down Apple's flailing arms and kicking legs while repeatedly stabbing him in the groin with plastic forks they'd confiscated during kitchen cleanup duty.

Scores of other prisoners—smiles on their faces—were gathered quickly to block tower guard vision of the gangster's final minutes. The prison medic was on his knees working over Solamenté's body.

As the Medic pronounced Solamenté' dead and that he died of natural causes, Tantrumatto was grinning ear-to-ear and so were most of those in the Courtyard below, both Guards *and* prisoners!

The Warden's next step was to cut off all access to prison phones and have the Medic report the death as accidental even though the Warden had little doubt that the circumstances would eventually surface and be questioned. He also knew all involved would support one another's reports on what happened.

‌ ‌

"So, Mike, does the Warden's news mean we're done with this case or just starting?"

Infusino shrugged, but looked left and right before answering his partner, Ron.

"Truth? Solamenté maybe started the whole deal and everyone's better off without him around, but, for openers, A) we don't know if he has or had a backup. B) the Mob Family here in Jersey may have some need for revenge at having their cage rattled. C) we don't know if who we've been callin' the Lobster Mobsters—those guys working in the Caribbean pretending to be cops—if they're still involved, or even connected, and D) we can't even begin to find those other slime balls who swam away from the original boat-sinking with bags of cash. E) So, long answer to short question!"

Ron responds, "Whew! That says it all. I guess we oughta take a break before any more tidal waves hit. Like at least take the wives out for dinner tonight, yeah?" Mike nods agreement with a pat on Ron's shoulder.

Chapter 34

Sortin' It Out Sort of...

"I am FBI Special Agent Randy "Red" Robbins. I have reached out to each of your commanding officers to recruit you as part of an elite nine-member military officer team that I've been asked to lead. I imagine each of you have been made aware of my background, but you may want to also be informed about the impressive background strengths each of you brings to our nine-member team table. Each of you are ranked among the eight best-qualified, most intelligent and experienced individuals in our home State, and in your specific branch of America's Armed Services."

Robbins scans the room. "I've requested us to gather here today to explain a special challenge that I need your help with and your commitment to." He pauses, steps toward the window, then turns back to face the eight high-end recruits. "Stop your brains and imagine for just one minute what positive, constructive things could be done with twelve and a half *million* dollars for those people in our county and state whose life savings accounts were scammed and who all desperately need physical, medical, emotional and financial help!"

He pauses, looks at the ceiling, then at each of the eight faces watching him. "Y'think we should just let it go its merry way in the hands of two rotten gangsters, named Gator and Charlton. These two guys rigged the receiving illegal-drug-delivery boat to sink so they could escape the commotion that cost a dozen lives, and then swim to shore with *twelve million, five hundred thousand dollars in cash*, and disappear? The missing cash, plus what was recovered, made it the biggest drug bust in U.S. history, and these two scumbags got away with it! And the word is they're still out there and they've still got the money, and living like kings!

"Remember the names I just mentioned: Gator and Charlton! They got away with the $12.5 million. It was never recovered from the deceased gangster Solamenté's $25 million total. That's *half* the damn money! And while our police and Armed Services have beaten their brains in to get back the first half, and nail those responsible, we've never found the drug-delivery boat or retrieved any of the cash."

Robbins steps back to glance out the window. "And most of this has hardly ever been mentioned," he says, then turns back to face the sixteen eyes and ears. "Not until now! We finally have a chance. We finally have some clues about where it is and how we might recover it!"

He paces the room as he speaks.

"I wanna go get 'em! I wanna get that money back into the hands of those who've been robbed, who've suffered the loss, who've had their bank accounts cleaned out, and many of them at times of desperate need, and headed into times of even more desperate need. You?"

Heads nod. Some jaws clench, along with more than just a fist or two.

"We're told that before Solamenté got his comeuppance from fellow-prisoners, he knew that these two dudes were holed up somewhere, rollin' in the dough he tried to steal, and that they were literally entrenched in the obscurity of some Caribbean jungle between

Belize and Panama which includes Honduras, Nicaragua, and Costa Rica! That's why I asked your commanding officers to have you meet me here!"

He uses a small tree branch to swirl a circle around the map of Costa Rica. Glancing at a map made the jungle area compare in size with combining New York, New Jersey and Connecticut, or California and Oregon. Even his well-traveled audience looked surprised at the geography.

"And that's why we each got special travel permits that allow us to carry our guns. We're gonna start here in Costa Rica." He taps the center of the map gently with his branch. "This is where these two bad guys were reported to be last seen nine or ten months ago.

"From all Seaport County Police reports, Chief John Oleson and the guy some of you may know, who just retired from serving as Chief for a couple of years before recruiting Oleson into that job, Lieutenant Douglas Axel Axe for short! report the following information.

"Word is that the two thieves who escaped the at sea drug transfer in a storm, managed to somehow swim away with the missing twelve and a half million dollars in cash when the receiving boat began to sink. We also hear these two slime-balls are greedy, bad-news bastards who have been living high-off-the-hog, are armed to the teeth, and are reportedly somewhere here in these thousands of miles of snake and insect-infested, mud-caked jungle between the Caribbean and the Pacific. Odds are they've settled in and are satisfied to not leave the security of their hideout."

He scans the eight faces. "We need to remember our purpose each day." Robbins pauses. "Even if we're lucky enough to be starting out in the right country, doesn't mean that this journey will be quick or productive."

He pauses, looks again at the map.

"We, Ladies and Gentlemen, are gonna find them, whatever that takes, because we're talking about a lot of needy lives—*your* friends, *your* families, *your* neighbors—that are hanging in the balance here. Whatever big chunk of the cash we're able to salvage can feed and cover survival costs for Seaport County and New Jersey State struggling families, abandoned babies, hundreds of handicapped poor people, ill and destitute senior citizens, and family-supportive working young people who can't afford college." Robbins pauses and looks to each face.

"Each of you, including Detectives Infusino and Focazio here," he points to them in the front row, "who helped us crack the Solamenté chunk of this story, were hand-picked for mental alertness, physical skills, creative-thinking, weapon-handling, ability to rise to the occasion and instincts for finding and apprehending bad guys like the pair we're looking for. And they, like each of you, also have strong military experience.

"In other words, all of you here are extraordinarily skilled and all nine of us have each had all the medical training, preventive drugs and injections required, and everyone in this room is ranked as an athlete and as a sharpshooter, so—a better team for this task could not be had. We are *it*!

"All right, here's the deal. The nine of us work together as three-somes at all times. We respect all natives, their families, and properties at all times. Remember it is they who could turn out to be our biggest asset because some of them, somewhere, will know where these dudes are holed up. And when we find that out, we quietly get on our Ham radio setups and get together quick without alarming anyone or mistreating any property.

"Once their location is confirmed, there can be no exceptions to the need for *only* the nine of us working together to get this job done. *Zero exceptions.* Got it?" Every head nods. "We do not need and do not seek any additional team members; we only need additional information as we go forward.

"Okay, y'all, three black, fully equipped Jeeps are outside with co-ordinated maps in each back seat. Let's plan to leave here together at zero five hours with one female driving the second Jeep and one in the back of the third Jeep.

"And, at least for now, no matter which Jeep you're in at any point in time you will keep the other two Jeeps within your vision every minute, and since we have no idea where this will all lead us, there can be no use of Jeep horns, got it? And again—*no* exceptions, yes?"

All eight heads nod in agreement.

☙❧

Coffee and donuts at the College Diner. "So, Chief," Axe asks, "what do you make of this kid we nailed climbing out of JP and the Professor's window, who we now have charges against for his unregistered gun, break and entry, grand theft, and Sarah Cranston's lab reports that the kid's been into some heavy coke use and twisted drug deals?"

"Hey, Axe," Oleson responds, "that's a pretty long question, but I would even add to that, the fact that the kid finally broke down and admitted he made that threatening three o'clock phone call probably means we'll be hearing from some representative of his father's pretty soon. A representative because his old man is undoubtedly a major Jersey Mob factor, Mafia Moneybags they call him. I'm told his name's Mario DePasqualini, from Newark."

"So, we need to be prepared for how to best handle this...lots of volatility here. The only good thing is that Solamenté's now out of the picture. So, I figure we're probably in a better bargaining position to get them to back off their pursuit of JP and Maddigan, y'think?"

Chief Oleson agrees as they sipped coffee.

"Well, Axe, besides that this diner should have Mrs. Obco's donuts, you got a point. We might get a better bargaining position, but y'know it's likely they'll just find some other avenue to follow, y'think?"

"Makes sense to me, Chief, especially the donut part," Axe grins. "Except, I'd hate to see the kid back on the street anytime soon. Breaking and entering, grand theft, carrying with no license, drug charges and who knows what else? How about we question him as soon as we get some more details on who he really is and what he's *really* all about?"

Chapter 35

Sounds like...?

"Sounds like a plan, Axe. I'll get an ASAP time to poke for more info. We don't want anyone postin' bail before we can question him. Can we delay bail posting?"

"I think it can be arranged. We can delay the earliest bail-post time, if there is any. I'm not even sure bail will be allowed once the judge sees how much money's involved, and gun-with-no-license, and sees my note about the kid's suspicious connections."

❧ ❧

"The girls called to ask if we'd come for dinner next Saturday night after they get back from New Hampshire and bring Flokie over to play with Bollen Y'think?"

"You don't even need to ask, girlfriend. I love your family almost as much as you, and—to top it off—Flokie's been askin' for Bollen. He told me he wants to bring his brother a bone! Does that work for you?" JP answers with a hug and kiss. Flokie licks them both!

໖৩

Maddigan answers the Abbey Beach cottage phone: "This is *Who?* Rico-as-in-Puerto"???

"Das ride," Rico responds, grinning ear-to-ear.

"Good Grief, Man! Those boat guys you introduced us to were *great!* We ended up in Puerto Plata, Dominican Republic, and now we're back home! And all's well! So, how *you* doin'? Are *you* okay? How'd ya get this number? What's goin on? Where are you?"

"Jeeze, alodda quesdions, Mon! Glad I Finally godsha! Ya harder da reach den da Presidend of the Unided Sdades, Mon. I been callin' lodsa differend numbers seems like forever. I been dryin' da led ya know... and JP. She's okay, yah? Anyway, do answer your "where" quesdion: I'm back add da Flocking Way/No Flocking Way indrasecshon an been dryin' da led ya know dad I heard aboud doze guys you mendioned who got away wid moocho money! Ya still wanna know boud dad?"

"JP and I are both good, Rico, thank you! And, *yes!* We want to know about those guys because what they did has caused all kinds of problems here, and we're trying to help find them, so whatever's left of the money that they took can be returned to the hundreds of people they stole it from, or if that's not possible, to use it to help needy families here."

"Well, Mon, soma da nadives here say doo guys named Gaddor an Charldon an dare girlfriends are holed-up deep in da Cosda Rican jungle—like some kinda Kings—in someding like whad dey call a fordress wid big walls dad dey had da nadivs build, and wid fulldime paid nadives as guards—sumpdin' like sixdy miles inda da jungle, nex do a liddle hidden river where dey keep dare moder-bodes for goin' do down every coupla munds do buy food and as many bags of cemend dad will nod sink da boad in da ocean. Plus drade-in sommada big cash dey gode for ones, fives, dens, and dwendies, and a buncha Cosda Rican Dollars. Den, day head fordy miles nord of down from where da river goes indo da ocean, y'know? I jusd wanded do led you and JP know cause you were bode so nice do me and da people I led you do ad da Flocking Way and No Flocking Way indrasecshon."

"WOW! Thank you, Rico! You do mean "intersection," I assume?" he asked, grinning.

"Das ride," Rico responded.

"Can you stay on the phone another few minutes so I can write down some of what you said? If you don't want me to tell anyone your name, I won't. But if it's okay with you, I will share it with a special friend who I promise will never tell anyone else? He's a special agent who I know will reward you big-time if the information you just gave me turns out to be right, and as long as you—or me and JP for that matter—don't repeat any of this phone call information to anyone else. Is that all okay with you?"

"Sure, Mon, I hold, and will also give you an address for me for da nex few munds!"

Maddigan grabs a pen and paper and gets Rico's full name and address, details on "da fordress" location, including that there are two to four guards and a cook present twenty-four-seven.

Rico explained as much as he could about the approximate location, and what he heard about the jungle they would need to go through. They arranged for a followup call in two weeks.

Maddigan then told JP about the call and that Rico was asking for her, which triggered a big grin from her. She asked to speak with him on his next call.

"Yup," Rick said, "But right now, I gotta connect with Axe, and get him over here pronto."

"Axe? Maddigan here. I just got info on the bad guys and the missing money you'll want to have to pass along ASAP."

"I'll be right there."

"Chief? Axe! Maddigan just got a call from a guy named Rico, in Costa Rica, who he and JP met in their travels. Rico gave him info on where the thieves and the missing money is. Can we meet with you now for a couple a minutes to fill you in?"

"How about over here, my office?"

"Gotcha. We'll be there in twenty minutes! Oh, by the way, you may want to let FBI Agent Robbins and Detectives Focazio and Infusino take a half-hour break wherever they are until you can get them the details."

"Thanks, Axe. See ya in a few."

☙❧

"Oh, Hi JP! This is Dean Oliviero calling. I was looking for Professor Maddigan to see when's a good time the three of us might get together again to catch-up on our plans for the new Communication Center."

"Hi Dean! Rick's not in at the moment, but I'll be sure to let him know you called as soon as he returns. He ran out of here just a couple of minutes ago. Is everything okay?"

"Absolutely! All's well! I just want to keep you both informed, and review a couple of questions related to semester timing and construction, ground-breaking ceremony, staffing plans, that sort of stuff."

"Well, we're definitely interested in all of that Can I put you on hold for a second so I can grab a pen and pad to jot some notes for him?"

"Absolutely!"

Ten seconds pass. "Okay, so I'm ready to write it down. Besides what you just said, Dean, what else can I relay to save you another call?"

"Great, JP! First off, I will appreciate the opportunity to meet that young man—Roy Flude, I believe? —who Rick mentioned was his prize student and the one he wanted to see as Student Radio Station Director. I just want to run through the details with Rick and you about how to get Roy on payroll."

JP smiles as she hears what she imagines is the Dean taking a big

175

puff on his pipe.

"Plus, I want to know who Rick suggests for Student Newspaper Faculty Advisor. I'm also hearing some questions from the College Planning Committee—which, by the way, is thrilled with your's and Rick's generosity. Bottom line is that we need to figure out the best fit for the new Communication Center with the newly-established campus Computer Center.

"We've had a lot of questions about how to best position the two buildings. I'm sure you know, for example, that the campus Computer Center uses one entire building-length wall for the new computer system. It's only the third computer in the whole State, you know? Anyway, the thinking is that we need to somehow make it be kind of a fit with the Communications Center."

The Dean pauses. "Oh! And I've had some thoughts too about housing some of those Anchor Out Personal Growth Group sessions you and Rick run. Maybe in the new building too, and maybe the College can pay you for working with some County residents who may have need for your help but can't afford tuition to qualify for the sessions. No rush to decide; it's just a thought.

"Oh, and you might want to know also that the SPCC Board of Directors is totally supportive of everything I just shared with you, including paying you both for the introduction of some supportive mechanism for your group sessions which they think could literally open a floodgate of community engagement with the campus. Anyway, how are you doin?"

She suffocates a laugh at his question after such an unsolicited outpouring of ideas and information that support the quest she and Maddigan have been dreaming about.

"Just Fine, Dean, and thanks for thinking of us about maybe running a few sessions in the new building and that whole Computer Center thing. Good food for thought! I'll be sure to have Rick call you as soon as he gets back. Have a great rest of the day!"

"Thanks, JP. You too!"

გ<del></del>ֆ

She no sooner hangs up and glances at her notes, and the phone rings again.

"Hi, this is JP." Laughter. "I know who this is, Big Sister! How ya dune?" Olee asks. JP grins ear-to-ear at hearing her little sister's little voice asking their Father's joke-gangster-accent question in as deep a tone as she could muster. JP copies Olee's voice.

"I'm dune just fine thank you, Olee. . . Wassup?"

"Well, we just got a buncha dog bones and Mom says I should check with you if we can give one each to Flokie and Bollen for the dogs' dinners Saturday night?

"A great idea, Olee. I'm sure both dogs will love you for giving them such special treats! We all like special treats to eat once in a while! And, that's a whole lot better than having them jump up onto the table and eat off your plate!"

They both laugh.

Chapter 36

The (Almost) Jungle Bungle

"Hi Chief! Rick Maddigan here. Axe said he was meeting you. Is he there? I just got some important info for the task force from a guy named Rico who JP and I befriended during our trek through Costa Rica. I thought you'd want to share it with your team."

"Hi Professor! Thanks for calling. Timing's perfect; Axe just walked in. Here, I'll put you on speaker phone."

"Greetings Axe! I just had a call from a guy named Rico who JP and I made friends with when we visited Costa Rica. He says that the two guys you and Chief Oleson said you're after, named Gator and Charlton and their girlfriends are holed-up deep in the Costa Rican jungle—living like royalty—in some kind of fortress with big stone walls that they apparently paid some natives to build.

"Rico says a couple of his jungle friends heard that they are also reported to have three or four twenty-four-seven native guards, who Gator and Charlton pay in—close to worthless—Costa Rican dollars, and have somehow managed to fully arm them with rifles.

"The guards are no doubt paid with American dollar-traded-pea-nut-amounts of the stolen cash that Gator and Charlton managed to swim to shore with when the Solamenté illegal-drugs-at-sea deal collapsed, due to crossed signals between Solamenté and the delivery ship captain.

"Anyway, Rico says he double-checked his close-friend sources who reported this hideout to be about 60 miles into the jungle. They told him it is located next to a hidden—almost unknown—small river which apparently doesn't even exist during times of low tide, and that's where Gator and Charlton each keep their own motor launch boats sitting in mud until the tide changes. It's adjacent to what Rico's friends say is their hidden living quarters.

"Rico's sources report that the two guys alternate themselves and their boats every other month to make these grocery and supply trips, and somehow manage to cash some of their big thousand and hundred-dollar bills for smaller—mostly singles, and a few fives, tens, and twenties, and a bunch of Costa Rican dollars. Most people there have only vague remembrances of one or the other of them and their boats, because each only appears in town three times a year to load up supplies—not uncommon in that area!

"Rico says most people there, even the store owners, have only vague recollections of one or the other loading their boats with supplies, and guesses that they likely eat native-grown fruits and vegetables and a lot of fish and snakes—no, uh, cows in the jungle!

"So, the Flocking Way/No Flocking Way intersection/marina and handful of stores is all that he says is around for like a hundred miles up and down the coast and inland as well. Bottom line is these two guys, and whatever's left of the millions of dollars they swam away with, are planted in this stonewall building about sixty miles inland in thick jungle, about forty miles north of town from where the river goes into the ocean, y'know?

"Anyway, Rico, who helped me and JP to escape back here to

the U.S. is honorable and can be trusted. He called us because, as he said, he just wanted to let us know all of this because he considers us friends and knows we've been trying to figure out where Gator and Charlton, were hiding out."

Maddigan pauses. He rubs his forehead to stay focused.

"JP and I want to suggest that if all of this pans out and our tough-military-police team you've described succeeds with this pursuit, and that Rico's information is helpful, that he be included in any thank you reward!"

Maddigan takes a long pause. "Okay, enough said. It's time to get off the phone and let you two communicate with your base team. Please keep us informed as much as possible as our guys move forward. And have a great rest of the week!"

"You too, Professor, and JP, who we assume is on the line?"

"I am, indeed, Officers! And thank you for all you do!"

"Great! Well, thanks for all that both of *you* do . . . much appreciated! We'll keep you posted, and thank you both for this call and the info. We been takin' notes. Catch you on the rebound!"

☙◈❧

"So whaddaya think, Chief?"

"Well, from all you tell me about JP and Maddigan, I made the judgment way back that they are honest to a fault. And I don't view any of what the Professor just said to even come close to anything less than 100% true. So, I think we need to get our long-distance emergency system up and running to transmit what we just heard to Red, Mike and Ron via their CB radio lines. We want to be sure that after they put all these pieces together with what they already know., that all their questions are answered."

"And while we got 'em..." Oleson says, "let's also be sure we request a callback with their mapped-out plan before they take another step toward that location, just in case, y'know? Maybe there's some way we can arrange sending additional resources their direction in case their plans call for any more than what they have, people, supplies, equipment, weapons, y'think?"

Axe gives Oleson a thumbs-up and salute.

⤝⤜

"Mom, I think these two brothers, Bollen and Flocky, are a lot like me and Pamela," says Olee.

Pamela adds a layer of support to her sister. "Yeah," she says, "they play tug--a-war with a piece of rope, but they eat together, sleep together and even lick each other once in awhile! But, uh, *no!* I don't lick my sister. Yucht!" They all laugh.

Saturday night dinner with the whole Haley Family, Joan and Pete and the girls and Bollen. JP and Maddigan appear relaxed for the first time in over a year, and Flocky is of course beside himself every time he's reunited with his brother.

There's still a little touch of rigidity about Rick and JP being away for the entire summer with no communication. But the circumstances that prompted that shut down have been becoming clearer, and the fact that Solamenté is finally a past-tense word, and that JP's youngest sister, Olee, unabashedly likes to hold Maddigan's hand whenever the family gathers, and even Pete and Joan unwind with a glass of wine, dog licks and the girls' laughter. The whole visiting experience continues to grow favorably on all of them. And JP couldn't be more pleased.

⤝⤜

"Okay guys, listen up!" FBI Agent Red Robbins commandeers the hotel room get-together of his nine-member task force, we're gonna try a tech breakthrough with a ham radio relay call from Chief Oleson with the Seaport County, New Jersey, P.D, and Lieutenant-partner Axe who's been actively involved, and who prompted this investigation trip.

"The two of them have come into some information that they think will help us find the bad guys, and will be calling us here with that input within the hour. You'll be happy to know that our Room Service Manager arranged air shipment of an actual award-winning feast of top-quality food from one of our chef friends stateside. It'll be landing here in the next few minutes, so make yourselves comfortable, and *max* by the way, you get one glass of wine or beer each. And it might be a good idea to get your notebooks out for the call!"

❧

The prison's new Solitary Confinement Prisoner arrangements now allow only one day a week for SCP's to have forty-five minutes of access to the courtyard, during times when only the guards are allowed access. During such times, their cells are sprayed with applications of antibacterial products from the ceiling fumigation system.

Phil Thee, Bo Strangles, and Chop Sooey—and any other prisoners who appear to be in regular groups—are specifically not permitted there at the same times, and all three former Solamenté associates—and secret killers—have been moved to four-wall, six by six cells with no bars and no windows. Food trays are passed through new wall slots that only guards can open and close. And guards are instructed to have no verbal or paper exchanges ever with any SCP's at any time, or face immediate pay suspension or loss.

Chapter 37

The Smorthering Jungle Journey and Campus Nwes Update

"It's another world altogether, both literally and figuratively," Robbins reported back to Oleson and Axe via dozens of static-filled ham radio relay transmissions. "So, I've got our team goin' slower than..." *Static.* "...we'd like to move, but we're..." *Static.* "...only gonna have one shot at..." *Static.* "...makin' this work, and that's only..." *Static.* "...gonna happen by extremely..." *Static.* "...careful observations and..." *Static.* "...listening in between blasts of..." *Static.* "...heat and rain and..." *Static.* "...bugs and..." *Static.* "...plenty of snakes. Coral Snakes, Tropical Rattlesnakes, Velvet Snakes, Black-Headed Vipers, Nocturnal Snakes, Palm Snakes. *All* can be fatal!" *Static.*

A long blast of static interruption, before Robbins' voice returns "It'll be a while before..." *Static.* "...we reconnect, but not to..." *Static.* "...worry. We're gonna..." *Static.* "...make this work." *Static. Click.*

"So, whaddya think of that Randy Red Robbins Report, Chief?"

Axe refills his coffee and grabs a second donut after hearing The Jungle Team's day two report.

Oleson, who had been walking in nervous circles around his desk, says, "Sounds to me, Axe, like we're in this for the long haul and it's maybe longer than any of us imagined, but I've no doubts about what Robbins or this nine-member team is capable of."

Oleson pauses to look out the window. "I *any* team can get through those jungles, arrest those two bastards and recover what's left of the stolen money, this is the one. And Randy (is exactly the right kind of leadership that can pull all this together."

He turns to face Axe,

"I just wish the mission wasn't so nerve-wracking and so damn far away, but I believe in these nine and what they're capable of. I know, of course, that you just wish communications were easier, too.. Maybe someday someone will invent a clearer, cleaner, more direct long-distance voice transmission system than ham radios, y'think?"

"Yeah, I do think, Boss, but, well, that's not likely anytime soon. I certainly agree we got the right combination of smart, tough team players out there and if anybody can cut through the crap and all that jungle and come back with a victory, they're the ones!"

❧

"Bottom line, Rick," says Dean Oliviero, "is that Dr. Stafford, who was replaced as President here by Dr. Davidson shortly after you first started teaching here at SCCC, never had the foresight or interest in the world of communications as a study program. But, Barry Davidson is a man of foresight and practical thinking, and he is why you have total Administrative support for your pursuits. We are all very hopeful of seeing this new Student Communications Center come to reality ASAP.

"Dr. Davidson is—and I can tell you this authoritatively—beyond thrilled for you and JP, that you have both stepped up to underwrite the construction expenses. In fact, I've worked with him now for twelve years, almost as soon as the college opened its doors—and even before he was named president—and I never heard or saw him so excited! He's convinced, as am I, that this new Center will literally put Seaport County Community College on the proverbial map, even give the State's big universities a run for their money!"

"Well, thank you Dean, and I'll be sure to relay your comments to JP as well."

Maddigan says, "I stopped in today to ask if you might be aware of anyone on our faculty or staff who might possibly be from, or know a lot about Costa Rica, y'know, topography, lifestyles, customs, value systems, family life, any of that?"

"Hmm, Costa Rica? I'm not sure, but will give it some thought. The only one I know off the top of my head is José Sánchez on our Faculty, who tells me his Uncle Oscar is slated to run for President of Costa Rica in a couple or few years."

"Well, José may be absolutely perfect. He's in the Language Arts Department, I assume? And can I say you suggested him to me? I just want to see if I can find out more that might help our local police team on a special mission right now."

"Absolutely, Rick, and tell him I volunteered him to see if he could help you!"

"Thanks, Dean. By the way, JP says you might be interested in having the new Center also serve to house some of those Anchor Out Personal Growth Group sessions she and I started on our boat. We both like that idea a lot and would be happy to discuss that possibility anytime that works for you. Just let me know."

Maddigan turns his back to the door.

"Oh, and thanks again for recommending contact with José. I'll give him a call this week. Anyway, I gotta run right now, but I look forward to getting together again soon. Oh, and please thank President Davidson for his interest and support. I'm hoping we'll be ready to meet with both of you sometime next week; just let me know a couple of best times. Have a great day!"

৵৹

Telephone message. *"Hey, JP! This is Katie. Thanks again for the great steak dinner! I missed you so much; it was wonderful to see you again, and I LOVE the 3-D framed beach house art you gave me. It's hanging over my home office desk so when I feel crunched with work, I can look up and daydream. Next dinner's on me. Love ya!"*

Telephone message: *"Ola, José! This is Rick Maddigan, Business Faculty. Dean Oliviero suggested you might have some info on Costa Rica? What's a good time for us to talk?"*

Chapter 38

We Can't Bungle the Jungle!

Agent Randy "Red" Robbins decided it was time to share an FBI bullet point Surveillance Report with his team. The report had been hand-delivered to him days ago as he stepped aboard his Newark, NJ, flight to Costa Rica. It was brief, to-the-point, and foreboding.

- *There's no road to the property believed to be occupied by Gator and Charlton.*

- *There's no road to where the so-called river meets the ocean; only handmade canoes and the culprits' motor launches go to and through that intersection. And only very rarely. The only thing less user-friendly than the mostly low-tide, mud river is the mud jungle to get there.*

- *Everything else for hundreds of miles north and east and forty miles south of the target location is thick with palm trees, and aggressive strangulating, often poisonous vines, thorny shrubs, dense thirty to forty-foot-high walls of bamboo, and strange, frequently poisonous creatures, especially snakes.*

• *Except for what some chopper surveillance photos show as a hand-ful of native grass huts scattered throughout the thousands of miles of jungle, and perhaps once or twice a year, a rare occasional tent, residences are virtually unheard of.*

Robbins calls everyone into a circle next to the three parked Jeeps, seemingly standing at attention on some semblance of a footpath, that periodically, requires the team to cut down seemingly endless clusters of bamboo and palm trees—without making any noise—in order to be able to proceed. Progress has been slow since they entered the jungle after dark.

They make no fires. Their floodlights are stowed inside Jeep tail-gates with batteries and weapons. They use blinking pocket penlights, posing as fireflies, to get around in the dark. The team has had to se-verely alter their sleep hours to start with full darkness and wake before sunrise, not even to mention serving guard team rotations.

They eat what they can, when they can, while bouncing over roots and rocks between tree clusters, rarely moving beyond five miles per hour, and frequently having to sweep dangling snakes of all sizes and poisonous ratings off the black Jeep canvas roofs with six, ten or twen-ty-foot-long poles they make out of thirty-foot-long bamboo cuttings.

Sitting together as the first touch of sunrise squeezes through the blanket of palm trees, Robbins addresses a huddle of his eight team-mates.

"Okay, y'all, listen up! He starts by reading the four FBI bullet points report then scans the eight pairs of eyes and ears locked on him before proceeding.

"We know what our job is. We know what the maps say. We know we're only a day or two or three from these guys and their hideout. Our teammates back home are diggin' up information for us around the clock, stuff we're gonna need to be able to do our job. We will be gettin' daily reports and information as we keep goin' forward. From all we know so far, if we continue to make this approach as we've started—in slow motion—we're probably lookin' at the day or two after tomorrow to execute our plan. What we have to zero-in on now, and tomorrow —and however much time it takes to process the info we get—is taking the best and safest way to find our destination, then get a better fix on what we're up against and then plan and execute our approach.

"We need to be 100% focused on *what* we learn going forward, on deciding the *best* way to get to our target, and determining how to best deal with whatever or whoever blocks our path. Then we must act! We must assess and implement how to best proceed once the two guys and the money are all within reach.

"Bottom line here, is that we got our work cut out for us, and every movement and every thought each of us has for the next few days cannot be addressed to anything else besides the focus of our jobs here, and, uh, remembering our prayers,if you don't mind my being a little parental at this point."

Robbins pauses to think.

"But, the truth is that we must each do everything possible to keep ourselves, and each other, 100% focused on the task at hand. And that means 100% teamwork!"

He looks pointedly into the eyes of each of the other eight faces.

"There's no room for goofing off, game-playing, daydreaming, talking, singing, whistling or even thinking about lovers or sports or families."

He pauses to let that thought sink in.

"We are here now for two all-important reasons *only*."

He scans the group to be sure of 100% attention.

One, to capture these two tough-guy crooks, while keeping ourselves safe and united as a family, and two, to retrieve every possible penny from the bags of cash they stole from our families, neighbors and friends and see that it's returned to benefit those families, neighbors and friends. There will be plenty of time, when this event is over and we return home with a victory and plenty of paid reward time off to discuss all the other stuff. So, for now," Robbins summarizes, "when a thought comes to the surface that is not directly-related to our mission here, tuck it away or make a quick reminder note for yourself, to bring that thought back to the surface once we've all returned to Seaport County. Got it? Any questions?"

No questions, grunts or groans, just affirmative and reinforcing nods..

☜☞

"So, Dad," JP said, staring into the telephone, "I'll appreciate it if you'll please share that news with Mom and the girls that we're now on a reduced alert program at the moment."

Pete says, "Well, that's good information to share! Anything more, JP?"

"Just that Seaport P.D. is apparently working with the FBI and they are now in the process of eliminating the risk situations we've all been subjected to. While we need to stay alert to any outside influences —meaning outside our families and friends, and the college—they've assured me that we don't need to lose sleep over or be worried about every phone call at this point. And Rick and I—and of course you, Dad— will have a very definite, detailed report from the police and special agents in the coming weeks."

"Well, that's a relief, JP; thanks for the update. I'll be sure to let your Mom, and your sisters, and Bollen all know."

"Great, Dad, and I guess I'd better let Flokie know too. I'll get Rick to talk with him, sorta mano-à-mano-à-dogo kinda stuff, y'know?"

Pete and JP both laugh.

☜☞

"José Sánchez? Hi! I'm Rick Maddigan. Dean Oliviero suggested I reach out to you for some Costa Rica information. I understand your Uncle Oscar may become Costa Rica's next president?" Maddigan says as they shake hands.

190

Chapter 39

We Can't Bungle the Jungle!

"Professor/Señor Maddigan. Is nice to meet you. My business students all have nice things to say about you. What can I help you with?"

"I've only ever been to Costa Rican mountains and resort areas. I've never been near the jungles, and was wondering if you could give me some rough idea of life there in the jungle, and what kind of income level there is for the natives who live there?"

Sánchez laughs. "Well, he says, there's not much life in the jungles there, and I'm not sure, but I believe that there's not any kind of income level. I've not had much experience with the jungle life there either, but those who I know who've dared set foot in that world of snakes and leopards and other not-so-friendly creatures, have told me there is very little human life in the jungles, except for occasional handfuls of natives who have grown up and survived there. Why do you ask?"

"It's part of a project I'm researching for some business contacts who are interested in investing in our campus plans down the road for a new Student Communications Center that's being planned, and that involves a couple of broadcasting test proposals that could possibly benefit some natives in Costa Rica and the Dominican Republic. I don't know a lot more right now. Just wanted to get some idea of possibilities. Anyway, I appreciate your time and input, and will keep you posted. Thanks, again."

They shake hands after chatting about a couple of star students, and Maddigan heads for the Administration Building.

Maddigan related the brief discussion in a quick visit with the Dean, who had urged him to be cautious in sharing information (since there was no way of knowing how close Professor Sánchez was—or is to his uncle or exactly when and where the FBI's task force would be in forward motion. After hearing Maddigan's rundown of the meeting,

Dean Oliviero responds, "Good job, Rick; not a lot of info there, but at least we can let the guys know they won't have to give up much to buy out the native guards and that the 9-member all-star team will have to be hyper-cautious in their approach. We probably ought to pass that info along to Axe and Chief Oleson ASAP."

∾∾

"Oleson and Axe for Robbins Jungle Team."*Static.*"Come in." *Static.*

"Jungle Team here, Chief and Axe! Gotcha!" *Static.*

"Right on time." *Static.*

"Whassup?" *Static.*

"Three things First, the prison guards are paid next-to-nothing. *Static.* Probably less a month than the biggest cheapskate on your Team has in pocket-change right now! *Static.*

"Remember the two names are "Gator" and "Charlton." *Static.*

"We hear you need to stay *very* alert for ocelots and jaguars, mostly at night. *Static.* and lotsa seriously dangerous snakes. *Static.*

"Roger on the jaguars, ocelots and snakes." *Static.* "And the pocket change info, and thanks" *Static.* "for the slimeball's names and the warnings. We only seen one jaguar at a distance. Snakes, yeah, everywhere." *Static.* "It'll be a while before we reconnect, but not to worry. We're gonna *Static.* make this work. *Static.*

"Roger that! God Speed!" *Static.*

"Okay, Team, Listen Up!" Red Robbins says. "First of all, thank you each for being here! Second, since y'all heard parts of our call with Axe and Chief Oleson, you know we need to be on full alert for jaguars, ocelots and snakes, and that the natives who are guarding the two thieves we're after, are getting paid peanuts. We'll pay them more to abandon those bastards and take over whatever the building and walls are all about, for themselves and their families. But, we've got to stay *very* careful and alert in the process! Let's all remember that—besides each of you being a superstar in your own right—the best thing we have going for us is the element of surprise!"

Eight heads nod!

"And we only use guns if there's no other choice! Understood?"

Eight more nods!

Chapter 40

Wishy-Washy Watchful Wading and Waiting

Swampy, unmapped, little streams run throughout the jungle floor around them, nourishing the wall-to-wall mud, shrubs, and trees, continually connecting one piece of insect-infested swamp with another and giving ongoing purpose to the entire reef as a jaguar nest.

Nights are black and days are dark but for rare spurts of sunshine that periodically seem to burst upon them before yielding to the domineering density of palm leaves.

Jungle undergrowth is home to half a million species of creatures—including tarantulas and 300,000 other insects—that seem to be everywhere and rattle with the winds and never seem to sleep, perhaps because of the Howler Monkeys, that howl continuously, are everywhere, and never seem to sleep.

Sunlight? The jungle canopy can be sixty to two hundred feet high—like a colossal, never-ending, multi-layer, palm-tree-blanketed forest.

That translates into extremely slow going for our three, three-person Jeeps. It feels like being endlessly stuck in the mud while having to contend with the constant presence of jaguars, ocelots, poisonous snakes, flat tires, and insects—especially tarantulas! It takes a full day of quiet path-clearing-tree-and-bamboo-cutting, just to go ten to fifteen miles.

Ongoing short meetings. One-on-one and all-together. Imaginations run especially wild in the never-ending heat and humidity, even in the shade. Physical, mental and emotional sweat dominates every minute!

And even with their repellent lotions and sprays, they are engulfed by insects of every description while mud and muck dominate almost every step, All the while they must be constantly on the alert for all the dangerous creatures that their presence attracts. Nine profusely sweating, mostly whispering humans, head-to-toe-covered in black hats, boots, and jumpsuits in ninety to a hundred-and-five-plus degree heat, pushes not only their nerve buttons, but those of scattering monkeys and birds as well, which of course attract bigger more threatening creatures.

Each of the nine must fend off the dangerously dominating daydreams of ice water, air conditioning, and cold six-packs. Each must accept the need to play as a flawless baseball team, with "Red" as both the star pitcher and their team captain.

There's no room for being loud, bitchy, or antagonistic or having second thoughts about the rare creatures, circumstances, and challenges to be faced in the coming forty-eight to seventy-two hours as they push forward, one step at a time toward their hidden target.

Red has them abandon the Jeeps, and continue forward on foot, wading their boots through the sucking muck and ever-thickening trees, shrubs, and threatening colonies of poisonous snakes. All with an edginess and fear of fierce wildcats that they don't dare to shoot at without giving away their existence to the culprits they are there to capture. Even with silencers attached, there's no way to know how close

195

someone they're looking for could be to hear the thump sound.

This step-at-a-time progress opens endless hours of stop'n rest sessions for quiet—often whispered—team discussions—to review maps, activate tracking devices, check gun silencer connections, determine directions to best-guess locations, and take turns listening to Ham Radio static for any possible input from home.

All of that, combined with prior training and daily plans, requires extremely careful steps—from turning and parking the vehicles to face back out to the cleared areas they created on their way in, to determining the absolutely essential gear to haul forward on foot to the still invisible target property, and deciding how to best transport back to the Jeeps any cash and bad guys they hope to be able to find and capture.

After another night of anxiety, the team resumes forward motion, rechecking their stun-gun silencers for just-in-case preparation of confronting threatening creatures in their path as they close in on their objective. And most importantly, the native property-guards in case they are not friendly.

Every member of the Recovery Team knows that above all other concerns and challenges they will have to exercise extreme patience in locating, waiting, watching, befriending, and if need be, capturing the bad guys' property guards to determine property details, approachability and receptivity.

They must do everything possible to gain the trust of the guards and ideally recruit their help in order to surprise and capture the target thieves, locate the money, and get safely back through the snakes, bugs and mud, to the Jeeps and be able to safely return back home to The States, and—of course—Seaport County.

⧉⧉⧉

Back home.

"Y'know, JP," says her youngest sister Olee, "ever since we got back home from the lake, Bollen's been like one of the family. Even

Pamela agrees. Is Flokie like that too?"

"WOW!" JP responds, "even Pamela agrees? Anyway, I'm so glad to hear about Bollen. And, yes! Flocky fits right in. He loves taking walks along the ocean and riding in the Jeep. I think he's even got Rick kinda wrapped around his paw. Know what I mean?"

"Well, yeah, JP, I know. It's like wrapped around your finger but dogs have paws, right? Anyway, we want to get together again soon. Can you talk to Mom or Dad?"

"You got it, kiddo. I'll call one of them tomorrow to see if we can set another dinner date—maybe here, our place? Then we can all walk along the beach to wade through the waves, collect some shells, and work up an appetite. You take care. Hugs to you and Pamela and Bollen. Tell Mom I'll call her in the morning about having dinner here. Kisses to you!"

Chapter 41

High or Low Tide Doesn't Matter When a Slice of Pie Is on the Platter

"All I know, Axe," said Chief Oleson, "is that after I called my old college buddy Johnny Armstrong —who's now California's new Governor—and explained what's been going on, he said he'd get back to me with some decisions he had in mind. I just hung up with him as you walked in here with coffee and donuts, and have I got news!

"Uh, maybe ya wanna take a sip and a bite first?" he asked.

Axe took a quick sip of coffee and grabbed a donut: "Go John! Wadda'd he say?"

"First off," says Chief Oleson, "Governor Armstrong relayed the info I gave him about what we've been dealin' with to our Governor here. And then, he acted immediately to relieve Tantrumatto of his Warden job. He put the two top Guards on probation notice that if they expected to remain on the job and be able to retire comfortably, they would have to do a closely-monitored 180° as Guards *and* as Enforcers.

"And listen to this, Axe! As for his Governor-to-Governor comments," Oleson continued, "his New Jersey call was filled with high compliments about the two of us and our teams, particularly as related to our diplomacy in dealing with Mafia channels.

"He—Governor Armstrong—also secured a pact—get this!— with our Governor here in New Jersey, ensuring that Mafia activists will also be closely monitored by a special National Prison Police Team they're launching to help ensure permanent, ongoing cooperation with Mafia organizations in both States. There will be strong restrictions attached, which he told me includes that any Mafia-based interference with State Police and/or Prison Police activities would result in bringing top State Mafia leaders into national spotlights in ways that would strongly and negatively impact their activities/relationships, and clout!"

"No shit! You think all that will actually make a difference and not be undermined?"

"Absolutely, Axe! I know the guy like family. It's what got him elected. Armstrong is not a BS'er... never has been, His track record speaks for itself!" Oleson pauses, smiles, then adds, "Uh, Y'think I can bite this donut now, Axe?

"Yeah, even two! And by the way, you can sip some coffee also!" They laugh.

ॐ•ॐ

Back in the jungle.

"Wassup, Boss?" asked Rick Alps, former USMC self-defense instructor, and one of the two dark-skinned officers on the Red Robbins' Nine-Cops Special Assignment Team.

"Hey, Rick. How's it going so far?"

"Piece a cake so far, Red. Wassup?"

"Just a question, Rick. Because we expect to reach our target in one more day, and hearing about your Marine background and smarts, plus you seem to me to be the number one machete champion here, having helped cut our way to this point—I was wondering if, ah...when we reach our target location you'd be willing serve as Advance Scout.

Robbins lets the thought sink in, then continues, "But before you answer, I'll tell you there could be great risk involved because success will only come if you can convince the first armed guard we find there that you are native to this jungle, that you are a good guy, and can work yourself into being accepted by one or two—possibly more—of the natives we hear are guarding our target residence. You don't need to answer now, but—"

"You got it, Red! Whatever you tell me we need to do, I'll do! Besides, I speak a little Latino and figure that being dark-skinned my-self helps. Plus, my years of self-defense and counter-espionage train-ing have taught me when to shut up, and what to say when something needs to be said." Rick continues. "I hear that the people who live here are dirt poor and live off the land, and that these two thieving bastards we're after are a couple of merciless scumbags who are nickel-and-dim-ing a handful of natives to guard them and their girlfriends. I was also, by the way, ranked first in my acting school classes so this whole deal is right up my alley. So, uh! What *is* the deal?"

The two of them move off to the side, away from the rest of the team. Robbins puts a reassuring hand on the Marine's shoulder and says,"You heard some of this before we left the hotel, but I'll clarify what we've learned so far. Understand, Rick, I have no way of knowing what to really expect when we find this place. Like if there's one or two or ten guards or whether it's enclosed by walls like a castle? Or if the tide'll be high or low. We don't know."

Robbins strokes his beard stubble, and takes a deep breath. "We don't know what the structure of the place is all about or how much area it covers, or if there's underground facilities. We don't know if these guys have a girlfriend each or ten each, or if these women are na-tives or imports, if there are any kids there, or if there are natives work-ing inside the place. We only know that any guards or employees are likely being paid peanuts. And we're going by the seat of our pants to locate the hideout, which could be made with sand-based concrete or cut tree lumber. It may have a wall around it.

"We know only that it is adjacent to a muddy low-tide stream that feeds into the ocean and that may only be navigable during high tide, which I understand is a rarity here. This area is said to be mostly low tide and muck. Here's my best guess of what to expect, and what role you'll need to play..."

Chapter 42

High Spirits & High Expectations

That night, Robbins held a quiet team-meeting of great importance. He explained the goal.

"To capture these two thieves with zero or minimal physical damage or upset *and* recover what's left of the money with minimal disruption in native lives, and minimal damage to whatever the facility or living quarters turns out to be."

Robbins then reviewed Rick Alps' U.S. Marine Corps and circus acrobat credentials with the others, and Rick's agreement to play the lead-man role of infiltrating the guard relationships and setting up a quiet relay system to clear the path while keeping us all informed and alert.

"This assignment," Robbins emphasized, "is *not* a piece of cake! And each of us must help make it work."

He pointed out that *if* the native guards could not buy into Rick's appeal, "allowing us to capture Gator and Charlton, and recover the missing cash without a big hassle—especially now, that recent discovery reports that these two guys were donating piles of cash to big name charities has proven 100% false!—then each of us has to be prepared for the worst in every sense of the word. Unlike football and hockey rules, you each and all have to be prepared to do whatever it takes to capture the bad guys and recover all the left-over money for the sakes of our needy and suffering neighbors, friends, and families, all the while being careful to *not* get shot, slashed, stabbed, clubbed, tortured, or burned at the stake!

"The cash," he adds, "is likely still in hundreds of banded packets of $500 and mostly $1000 bills and is fairly certain to be buried or hidden away on the property. The guards are unlikely to know anything about it or where it's hidden, and probably have no idea of the value vis-à-vis their own Costa Rican dollar, which is less than zero compared to our Benjamin Franklin hundred-dollar bill.

"So," Robbins continues, "the first goal is to befriend one or two property guards who we first encounter once we can locate and spot the property. Let's remember that the guards are *not* our enemies, and that we are on their land!

"We hope to befriend and meet quietly with them to explain that the inhabitants living there are not paying or treating them fairly, and that the money they are being paid was stolen from needy families. We will pay the guards much more than they are currently getting and we will leave them with legal ownership of the property and two boats and all, to use as they choose.

"Remember," he adds, "The better we are at doing this, the less likely we are to have to battle our way back out of here to get home. So, with everyone's teamwork, we'll be able to accomplish all of that."

Robbins and Alps nod agreement to one another.

"Keep in mind—every minute—throughout all of this who it is that we represent, and that the burden of success is on the shoulders of each of us. Each of us is responsible to one another. And we are also each responsible to all those who are suffering right now because of these missing funds—from the hungry and homeless to the infants and seniors and many in need of unaffordable immediate medical care and attention—and, for some of us here, that includes friends and family members.

"Above all," Robbins points to each of the eight faces, "Remember, there is no room here at *any* time for *any* of us to drift off mentally, or to not exercise courtesy or commitment or physical, mental, and emotional strength during every single minute of the next few days while we are here, and on our way back home.

"I remind each of you that you were selected from among the strongest and best-skilled members of the United States Army, Navy, Marines, Airforce, Coast Guard and Border Patrol. And you may never have another chance in life to make such a big difference on the side of doing the right thing for some of our country's neediest people. So, stay close to your prayers," Robbins ends his speech, "and remember your commitment to make a difference!"

∂∾✑

Back home.

"Remember to say your prayers, Olee," reminds Joan Haley as she tucks in her youngest daughter, "and you should have extra nice dreams tonight because we are all going to JP and Rick's cottage for dinner tomorrow, and yes, we're bringing Bollen too!"

"Oh, WOW! That makes me so happy to dream about, Mom, all of us getting together again. And if it's nice out, maybe we can go a little early so we can all walk Bollen and Flokie on the beach? Maybe it will even be, like, low tide, so we can find some shells? Maybe we can..." She yawns.

"Yes, dear, that would be nice, and we will try to do that! You have a good sleep. See you in the morning!" Joan kisses her daughter's forehead as she pulls Olee's cover up to her chin, then turns to leave the room. As she closes the door, Olee snuggles and says, "Thanks Mom!"

❧❦

"So, we're all set for tomorrow's family dinner visit?" Maddigan asks JP.

"Well, I imagine we are, especially since Mom just called to ask if it'll be low tide so we can walk the dogs on the beach and collect some shells," JP chuckles at relaying the message to Rick.

"Sounds like a plan," he laughs. "And what a stroke of luck!" he exclaims, as if he was on-stage in his classroom. "Low tide tomorrow, as it turns out, is exactly an hour before you and Flokie scheduled our dinner. Will that interfere with food prep time?" he asks with a grin.

"Hell, no, I was just gonna order pizza!" she replied laughingly.

He scowls. "Just kidding!" she adds, "The girls would love it, but my Mom might never come back, and no! No interference with prep time, but it may create havoc after dinner and dessert, and after they head home, and you and me maybe return to the beach for an after-dark dessert!"

He asks "Uh, Rum?"

"No," she says. Yum!"

They laugh and hug.

❧❦

Back to the jungle.

"So, what did you two actually do to untangle that Solamenté guy from the Jersey Mafia?" Red Robbins poses the question to Focazio and Infusino, as they sit huddled in the darkness, leaning against one of the Jeeps. They'll leave all three vehicles behind at sunrise. Both FBI Agents squirm, hunch their shoulders, and smile.

As they are about to answer, Navy Lieutenant Roger Ringland, the other dark-skinned team officer along with Alps, sits down next to the three of them, excuses himself for interrupting, and says he needs to ask something important. The three lean in to hear his question.

Roger reaches to shake hands and introduce himself, an experienced acrobat before joining the Navy. He says Rick urged him to interrupt the FBI trio to share some thoughts about why both he and Rick think they would be ideal partners for the first encounter with any guards. Because Roger, it turns out, had considerable experience applying his acrobatic skills to special escape projects as part of his preventative training services that he exercised often to ship-and-submarine-bound Sailors.

"And obviously," he adds, "Rick's and my dark brown skin will likely offer an initial comfort-zone match with any of the native Guards."

Roger proceeded to explain his military training focus on dealing with panic management and implementing creative escape techniques for special application in sinking/collision events.

Their discussion continued for well over an hour as Roger offered many examples of what he felt could be a useful partnership arrangement with Rick, and with one of the two female members of their team, U.S. Air Force Captain Audra Kelly, who he had once met years ago at a military Acrobatic Competition session where she was a featured tightrope walker.

He said he thought this combination—along with Rick—would maximize their chances of winning submissiveness as they approach a Guard or Guards.

They brought Rick and Audra into the discussion to map out a number of alternative plans using the Roger and Rick as front men, and Audra as the magnet to attract the interest and attention of any guards.

There was no question about this being the best route to follow. Robbins, Focazio and Infusino agreed wholeheartedly with Rick and Roger. They invited Audra into the discussion, and she was cranked to participate.

Chapter 43

Hummin' and Drummin'

Robbins made Rick and Roger's and Audra's scouting plan "official" once he heard them share their thinking and diverse experience, and then "passed the word" to the remaining team members, in between their quiet sleep attempt snorts and snores.

As Robbins, Alps, Ringland, and Kelly ended their discussion to get some sleep, none of them had any doubts about hearing distant drumming, or realizing how close they were to the source of their target. Word of Red's plan circulated with the rest of the nine-member team to proceed to a hidden, distant point that would usher them into the jungle-hidden encampment with a carefully detailed action plan for Rick, Roger, and Audra to initiate invasive steps at sunrise.

❧❧

Back Home

"Wow!" exclaimed Olee, "I really love to watch Bollen and Floki run into and along the low-tide edges. They look so happy to be playing together again. Y'know, they almost look like they're smiling? And their golden fur looks so much darker when they're wet!"

"I couldn't agree more, young lady," responded Maddigan. "Me too!" JP chimes in.

"Well," adds Pete, "I imagine by the time we get back to the cottage, they're gonna need some good dry-toweling off to keep us all from running away from the table while they jump into our places, shake off the salt water and eat our dinners," which he accented by his dih, dih, dih, dup, ta-dah, humming, and finger-tips drum roll against the shirt covering his chest, which he repeated five or six times! They all laughed.

୭∾ଓ

Back to the Jungle

Encouraged by the rest of the team's support—especially all the back pat comments—from Robbins, Infusino and Focazio... Rick and Roger and Audra whisper "If this / then that" plans to each other as they sprawl out, sitting on small Army tarps, and leaning against the equipment and supplies piles that rested on cross beam bamboo poles. Most of the others sleep about twenty feet up ahead, closer to the peaceful sounding thumps of the distant drums.

Neither Rick, Roger nor Audra—the Advanced Scout Trio—nor any of the others—have even the slightest idea about what to expect to find as a structure. They haven't a clue if it's part of the boat/stream area or not, whether the closest ocean and stream water levels are now high tide or low tide, etc.

They have no advance knowledge of how many Guards they may encounter—or where any other off-duty Guards may be, whether they carry rifles and/or pistols and/or swords—hopefully, swords—where they might expect to find the two "bad guys"—Gator and Charlton—and their wives or girlfriends. Hopefully, they're all be asleep in bed.

But bottom line is that they need to assume there are numerous off-duty Guards, that everyone there has high-end guns, and that everyone's "up and around."

The decision that they all agree to is first, to approach the target facility and Guards in early morning, calmly, pleasantly—slowly and quietly—and depending on what their first visual, by power-binocular scans and/or verbal, by camouflaged belly-crawl 2-way radio whispered "scout" reports turn out to be—each American team member will be charged with a specific set of responsibilities to carry out.

After agreeing that automatic rejection—and possible gunshots!—could be triggered by appearing "too clean," Alps and Ringland and Kelly decide to beat up their sandals and shorts with pocketknives and to "muddy-up" their skin to look "jungle-authentic," especially blonde, fair-skinned Audra.

Rick looks up after each of them creates a variety of "mud-smears" on their necks, chests, faces, foreheads, arms, legs and feet. "Okay, Rog, so waddaya think we do now?"

Roger responds, "Well," he laughs, "keep your distance from soap and water for the next few hours!" They all laugh. "Bottom line," he continues in a more sober tone of voice, "is that we need to figure out the best ways to think and act. We need to always be conscious of what our purpose is, and not allow the element of surprise seem or feel like a surprise."

He pauses and looks at their "muddied-up" skin again. "In other words," he says, "We need to be convincing enough to make what we want to happen actually happen. We need to win over any of the Guards and servant staff members we meet and to do that by being respectful of them and by pleasing them. Once they accept us for our skills, friendliness and sense of worthiness that the three of you create, we'll be able to count on one another as teammates. That will open the door for the rest of our team to apprehend the two bad guys and reward each of the Guards and servant staff people with more money and property rights than any of them ever even dreamed possible—y'know whaddamean?"

"In other words," says Rick, "We need to act and proceed with—and communicate promptly—that the mindset is as it should be. That we need their help to capture these two bad guys and return them to the U.S. means we need to be keeping the thought in the foreground of every word and action that while people may not necessarily buy what we do. They will definitely buy why we do it, meaning it's for them to see that what we do is to their personal advantage—including, of course, the jail terms the U.S. plans to deliver to their two bosses!"

"And," adds Roger, "we need to keep focused on that mindset because success will come from knowing that we have the skills and wherewithal to make it all happen for the good of all concerned, and all we need is their help!"

Rick nods agreement then continues, "Any and all Guards we encounter must be made to feel receptive to our plan because they will make more money and end up with a substantial piece of property that they can legally own and share and do whatever they want with. And that includes the two motor-powered launch boats and not have to answer to these two American bad guys, or to anyone else! AND most of all that, in fact their own Costa Rican Government agrees with the plan!"

Rick adds, "The plan is that these two bad guys we take back with us will finally be held responsible for stealing money from poor, starving, needy people they robbed in order to get here and selfishly control the jungle that belongs to the Guards and their families and their tribal community.

"That's the short version, but that's pretty much what I believe we have to communicate to these people. We must take every opportunity to convince them that we are here for them and to take these evil intruders back home to be punished. In the process, we'll give each of the native Guards and/or servants ownership and control of the facility, plus hundreds of U.S. dollars, which translates into a great many thousands of C.R. dollars, for food and supplies for their own families.

"We have no way of knowing the actual likelihood of them being aware of anything that has to do with the location of, or amounts of, money involved. We'll need to start with the mindset that they have no idea about anything that has to do with the money involved, including amounts and locations of the hidden cash!

"Once the reward potential seems acceptable to them, we need to spell out all the details and make a show of force with having them escort us and our captives (and, quietly, the cash we are able to find) back to our Jeeps.

"If the two Americans—and/or their guest females and/or any of the Guards—make a show of arms, we must be prepared to attempt reasonableness and then, if all else fails, we may need to shoot our way out and back to the Jeeps."

"We need to remember that we are here for two reasons. To capture and return with the bad guys, and to find and return with whatever money remains that we are able to find. But—most importantly—we must remember that we cannot get answers to money location questions if we or the Guards kill both bad guys!"

Chapter 44

Up before the Daughters & Up Before the Sun!

Back Home

"Mornin' Pete!" says JP's Mom to JP's Dad. "Olee and the girls are still asleep. That was quite a busy, fun-filled night last night. Besides the ten tons of exotic sea shells we collected, what did you think of it all?"

"Good morning, Joan! Yeah, I thought I heard some mornin' snorin' as I tip-toed my way down here for a cup of coffee. Good thing it's the weekend or we'd all be late for school. Last night? Hey! That was fun! I enjoyed the beach walk with all of us and the two dogs runnin' in and out of the low-tide waves as much as I enjoyed that meal JP put together and chatting with Rick, and seein' you smile so much. You do have a great smile, y'know." She smiles at her husband's pleasant response.

"What did you think?" he asks.

"Fun! Fun! Fun! It reminded me of times when we first met, and took long walks along the beach after dinner. Remember those?"

"Yup! I call 'em fallin'-in-love days." He winks at her and then takes a deep breath. "Maybe it'd be a good thing for us to be doing those long walks again? Sure beats watchin' TV!" He sees her smile, and asks, "So, you think we're on our way to add our first son-in-law to the Haley Family?"

"No doubt about it, Pete. And I think that would be as great an idea as your suggestion to start taking beach walks again!"

He grins ear-to-ear. "Yup, and don't forget, we just added our first golden retriever to the family, so—"

"So," she finishes his sentence, "maybe they'll both deliver gold to us?" she says, smiling, then laughs.

He laughs back.

She follows with, "It's a blessing to see how much they care for one another. Uh, JP and Rick—as well as the dogs, of course! And," she accentuates with a playful punch on Pete's shoulder, "considering even the small amount of what we know about what they've been through together already, and how Olee is always trying to hold Rick's hand, I think he's going to be a charming addition to our family. And, no doubt he's also a top-notch teacher!"

"Morning, Mom! Morning, Dad!" Pamela enters the kitchen. "I had a really nice time last night; y'think we'll be able to do it again soon?"

"Yes, Pamela, your father and I were just talking about that. It certainly was a fun night. Yes, I'm sure we'll do it again soon. Maybe here if I can count on you and," she gestures up the stairs with her head, "your little-miss-sleepy-head-sister to help with setting the table and making dessert and clean-up? Whaddaya say we shoot for the weekend after next?"

"Sounds like a plan, Mom. And I'm sure Olee will be pleased too!"

❧◆❧

Back to the jungle

"Okay, Y'all, the sun's coming up! Time to wake-up and let's get some food and coffee into you! Sunrise is on the way, and we need to review our plan and our back-up plan, to make sure we're all on the same page, and so that there are no unanswered questions."

Each of the other five members on the nine-officer team (besides Red, Rick, Roger, and Audra) know what they are supposed to do, and when, and how, and what to do if this happens or that happens, or nothing happens.

Each has experienced similar one-on-one and team dynamics but not in a jungle, and not with so much at stake—both lives and money—so they listen attentively to their leader.

"Rick and Roger and Audra," Robbins whispers, "will make first contact. Their task is to ferret out the first Guard or Guards they find, represent themselves as jungle life, and be able to explain enough to get some response and information about where the bad guys we're after actually are, and about the place, about the other Guards, maybe even inquire about job-possibilities. They will use that platform to determine how many other Guards are on duty and when's the "Changing of the Guard", and try to learn who exactly is in the facility and where-in the facility, and—if possible—try to determine how much they are paid as Guards, and what hours or shifts they work.

"Oh, and don't yell, gasp, or applaud if and when you see Roger do a couple of circus tricks he's developed for this encounter, or Audra tiptoeing across the treetops. Roger is, after all, a talented circus performer as well as a great Navy officer and Audra is an experienced and talented tightrope-walker. Think of Rick as Master of Ceremonies. The rest of us all need to stay quiet as mice for all of our sakes!

"In the event that this doesn't go well, one will signal the other six of us to quietly move in while they do their best to engage and distract the Guard.

"Watch me for if and when to move in. Remember, if any of

you get to the point of having to make a choice—it could be a turning-point decision—depending on how our initial face-off plan might happen. In the case of an irretrievable option, it's still going to be better to wound than to kill."

Robbins continues. "Here's why. Remember, we still need to locate, uncover, find the cash-stash, which—besides hopefully finding and returning the stolen money—is half the reason for being here. It could be in luggage bags, boxes, metal or fireproof containers, or even just buried in dirt, sand or cement.

"The point is this. These two scumbags have stolen and are hiding twelve million U.S. dollars IN CASH that we need to recover whatever's left in order to help the many sick, hungry, destitute families, friends, and neighbors in our home base Seaport County area who are struggling right now—today—to make ends meet.

"It's even likely, as a worthy reminder, that members of your own families, or friends and neighbors could be included in this mix.

"Odds are you'd probably be shocked if you took inventory of people back home who are working beyond-belief hours and/or back-breaking tasks just to survive. Just to put food on the table. To afford an aching tooth repair or serious medical treatment that they don't have insurance coverage for. Or who are simply scared at the thought of losing their jobs or living from their modest savings accounts. the friends and families who are just barely surviving the economic crisis brought on by gluttonous self-serving Mafioso!

"And, NO, I am not suggesting that all Mafia members are necessarily bad guys." Robbins adds, "But this particular amount of money and these two particular gangsters ARE, in fact, in it up to their necks! And they are, therefore, ultimately responsible for enormous suffering by thousands of hard-working, well-intentioned neighbors, friends, and families of Seaport County, and the entire Jersey Shore—and probably the rest of the State as well for that matter!"

He takes a slow deep breath, prompting others to do the same, as he heads toward finishing his Pep Talk.

"I know you know, but it bears repeating. These two guys we're after stole the money! Much of it was lifelong family savings. And we have the chance to get them, and get the money back, and be able to return it to the thousands of needy families at a point in time that it will make a dramatic difference for all of them! AND, for which we will regulate, share and ensure fair returns to the victims.

"What we don't know is whether these creeps are living with their wives or their girlfriends, but—either way—it's obviously an anticipated life of endless cash to do what they want—except travel—at least for now, until time takes away the heat, if you know what I mean.

"So, we befriend and payoff the Guards. We capture the two guys and find the money. We help the female partners to move along in life. And, we keep ourselves safe and protect one another until we are back home with the bad guys and the cash!"

Robbins pauses and looks in each face before concluding.

"Okay, officers, staying calm in our final approach to solving this problem here within the next couple of hours, is the secret to success."

He smiles and stands. "So," he says, "I'm going to share a breathing approach with you that I've learned and that works to keep you calm and focused! If you already know it, then consider this a reminder." He looks around at the eight attentive faces. "It has helped me thousands of times!"

Chapter 45

Are You Breathhing?

Red Robbins starts the day whispering to a quiet gathering of his team. "Please listen first, and then we'll do it. Here's how it goes:

"Each of us will close our mouths, and in our minds, say to ourselves, *Healing Energy IN* as you quietly inhale a deep breath through your nose, and down through your chest and push it down into your stomach—so your stomach sticks out instead of your chest—and then hold it there for 5 or 6 seconds. Then push your stomach in as you bring that air back up to your chest and hold it there for a couple of seconds then exhale quietly and gently through tightly pursed lips as a smooth, slow, steady stream through your mouth.

"Do this as you think to yourself, *Energy IN. Stress and Tension OUT!* And making sure that you push out every possible bit of air, before inhaling again and repeating the process a couple or three times, or more if possible.

"Okay. How about we all stand up and take a couple of deep breaths together here and now, and let's be thankful for each other's support and that we've made it this far. Remember you can do this silently, anytime you feel nervous or anytime you are about to approach a difficult or dangerous challenge, and even when you find yourself in the middle of a struggle.

"Oh, and it's a hellava good thing to teach your families after we get back home! Yup! It works for ALL ages!"

☙◆❧

They all stand and follow Robbins' lead as a first glimpse of sunrise peeks through the palm tree top openings. The nine of them take three deep breaths each before spontaneously gathering quietly into a circle. Then, spontaneously, without even another word spoken, nine right-hand-palms-down extend into the center of the space they surround and physically mount the other right hands atop one another, where they hold their hands—steady, atop one another—as Robbins says a short blessing.

Then, they all break and assume their individual assigned positions ready to inch forward in the heavy humidity and insect-infested mud and shrubs, intent on reaching and achieving their goal without making any unusual sounds.

Rick, Roger, and Audra are wearing faded, torn, patched denim shorts, along with their "homemade" gauged, dirty sandals and dirty torn t-shirts.

Rick and Roger have scruffy short beards and carry wooden-handled, muddied-up machetes. Roger has a fourteen-inch "Bolo" blade machete and a small beat-up-looking leather waist-belt pack; Rick has only his eighteen-inch "Bush" blade.

Audra has muddied and roughed-up her hair, face and skin. She carries a killer-large switchblade knife in a dirty leather holder that's roped through the belt loops on her shorts. She carries a lengthy rope over one shoulder. She and both men look strong, but friendly.

Rick and Roger's machetes dangle, as loose tools, off rope belts.

Rick quietly hums a "jungle song" he learned from an African lion-tamer he met in his traveling circus days. They walk quietly in step as they approach what appears to be a rough-surfaced, well-hidden, eight-foot-high, sand, cement, rock wall hidden behind shrubs and palm trees.

It's 9:30AM jungle time. The sun is already baking hot. "Hey! Who you?" a shrill native voice calls out from the closest wall-top corner.

"We be from Panama workin' tru here to find Granada!" Roger responds with a smile.

"Gothotherway!" the Guard whispered loudly and gestured with a beat-looking old rifle after a quick head turn to apparently check out if he'd been too loud.

"We gothotherway, but got no water. Can we getta drinkawater?"

After no response, Rick launched into an acrobatic stream of movements, including a famous "Leapinlizards" somersault-jump-series he invented, that never failed to fill circus seats. In fact, two nearby chimps stopped dead in their tracks from continuing to swing on some nearby vines in order to watch. The maneuver, highlighted in this case, by a breath-taking slanted-palm-tree-speed-climb and series of flips that landed him just ten feet from the eight-foot wall, with him juggling his machete with a pineapple!

While Rick has the Guard's full attention, Audra climbs an adjacent tree and with Roger's quick help strung her rope from there to another tree thirty feet away. She then began her tightrope walk and acrobatic dancing antics just as Rick did his machete-pineapple juggle finale.

Roger speed-walked to Rick's rehearsed landing spot while the performance distracted the Guard. The three of them ended up standing together and smiling at the Guard, who turned his head away again and then back to them, also with a smile.

"Dasome-goo-trix, Mon!" he responded. Still smiling, he shook his head and gave all three a look of amazement, then nodded his chin up and said, "Wade heer!"

Minutes passed. It felt like an eternity to the three of them—and, of course, to the three binocular viewers, Robbins, Focazio and Infusino—all hidden from view and from sunlight reflection in the jungle camouflage.

Finally, the Guard returned. He came down the steps with a jug of water and another Guard who wanted to see Rick and Audra do a repeat performance. After guzzling the water, the pair repeated their performances to smiles and quiet applause from both Guards. Then the two Guards gestured to Roger, Rick and Audra to stay where they were. The Guards moved twenty feet around the wall-corner to huddle and, as they managed to explain to the visiting trio of performers before stepping aside, *to talk about an idea we have.*

When Audra was sure no one was looking, she gave Rick a quick arm-punch and smile. "You were great!" she whispered. "Absolutely fantastic!"

Rick whispered his reply, "Yeah, I was sure as hell better than that water they gave us, and you, Dear Captain Audra, were equally amazing," Rick whispered back, as he dumped what was left of the water reward in a nearby shrub, then kicked sand over the small puddle that appeared. The three of them grinned. Roger turned sideways to flip a quick thumb's up toward the binoculars.

The two Guards returned at 10:30 to tell Rick and Roger and Audra, "Our dos Hefes and dos amigas would like to meet the tres of you in one hour for a Comida show. Like U dood for us. Is good?"

Rick and Roger both nod as they respond, "Con mucho gusto!" All four of them smile and nod. The two disguised natives give the two Guards thumb's up gestures.

"So, quatro personas?" Roger asks)

"Si Dios quiere," says Guard #1

"And you ambas? Otra mas Guards or staff?"

"No mas Guards? Solamente dos!"

Roger grimaced, unnoticed, at the name association. "El guiser?"

"Si, El guiser... is bueno!" Roger replied with a smile.

The Guards then escorted the three of them to a small shaded area along the wall to a corner closer to the entrance, brought them more water and urged them to stay where they were and to rest. And the Guards hinted that if all went well, all three of them would be well-rewarded.

Once they were out of earshot and line of vision from the Guards, Rick and Audra began working out a performance plan while Roger figured out a "Guards blindspot" location that appeared to be in line with the rest of the Team's three binocular users.

Roger proceeded to explain in sign language, as he quickly and quietly faced the binoculars, what was being planned. He urged them to "sit tight" but be prepared for the lunchtime show, and communicated it may be the perfect opportunity—while the two thieves and the two Guards and the cook are preoccupied—to sneak up to the back of the complex, and quietly find another entrance—or scale the wall with ropes if need be—to search for the money. while a couple of other team members stay keyed-in nearby to capture the two "bad guys," hopefully soliciting help from the Guards.

The Guards and the cook will have to be snagged and disarmed in as friendly a manner as possible, by Rick, Roger, and Audra, then taken aside for a full explanation of what the deal will be, including that each Guard will be given some huge amounts of cash, plus full ownership of the property to do with as they wish, and that the two girlfriends will be let go for the Guards to decide if they want to help them, or simply send them on their way.

And, reasoned the performing one-third of the American Team, Rick, Roger, and Audra in the unlikely event that even if the two thieves should manage to get away yet again. It's unlikely they'd get very far considering that it happens to be low tide at the moment according to the charts that they picked up before heading into the jungle.

So," the three of them conclude, "there's no way these two guys can jump into a boat. And unless they have a hidden helicopter ready and waiting, odds are that the only "escape" path for the two crooks is either to run straight toward the fully-armed American recovery team or go farther north into much denser and much more foreboding jungle than the three Jeeps and the nine of them experienced in getting to this point. Even all that money can't buy Jeeps like ours in the middle of this jungle, or find and follow a path like the one we createdor any kind of escape route!

The bottom-line risk here for all, they agreed, is in getting shot and having no medical support or even access much beyond basic first-aid skills. And the second big risk to the challenge at hand is having to be manipulative and or physical if they get no cooperation in locating the stolen millions of dollars.

ॐॐ

Back Home

Locating the new Student Communications Center building adjacent to the SCCC campus's two-year-old Computer Center is, according to Dean Oliviero, "A match made in heaven for the people of Seaport County."

"It'll be built there," the Dean notes, as he addresses the college's Board of Directors, "because it's almost exactly in the center of the campus, which is exactly in the center of the county. And it will provide print and broadcast, county and campus-based news as well as serve to attract and inform our students, student-families, faculty and guest speakers and presenters, along with area businesses and educational-based programs and both charitable and educational-based organizations for years to come."

Dates and details for the building commemoration, ground-breaking and dedication programs and ceremonies will, according to the Dean, be announced shortly. Dean Oliviero predicts all-time record attendance numbers for those events.

Chapter 46

Puttin' on a Show & Findin' the Right Moment to Act!

Back to the Jungle

Gator and Charlton and their girlfriends have yet to show, but another Guard—the third, and most senior—has arrived with a sub-machine gun over his shoulder and the woman who must be the cook and apparently either his wife or girlfriend, standing behind him. They stand off to the side of what's been designated as the stage area, talking quietly with the other two Guards.

The machine-gun Guard leaves the woman and the other two Guards to approach Rick and Roger and Audra—clearly scanning Audra's slim-trim appearance.

"Buenos Dias! My men say you guys do some acrobat act? They told the bosses to come see it. Where you from and how'd you get here?" he asks with an arrogant chin-up, authoritative but doubtful whine and one hand on his gun. Roger makes a mental note of the Guard's almost perfect English and quickly double-checks to make sure that all of them are in ideal alignment with the binocular viewers, before answering.

"We be here from Dominican Republic by boat to Panama Canal and working our way to Belize for jobs at Jaguar Reef Lodge. We got lost in the jungle coming from Flocking Way and No Flocking Way and came this way by mistake, but then we saw your Guards and gave them a sample of our skills so they would not shoot us, and so maybe we could get something to eat besides coconuts and pineapples.

The "Boss Guard" dropped his hand from the gun and laughed. "Well," he said, "I'm quite certain we can get you something better to eat than just coconuts and pineapples, assuming you put on a good performance," he added with a slightly threatening smirk, then nodded over his shoulder. Here comes dos cuatro bosses," as the two men, both packing pistols, and a girlfriend each, appear at the front steps.

The Boss Guard turned and walked briskly to the steps to fill in his "four bosses" on the briefing he just had and show them to their front-row rock-and-bamboo seats. The cook and the other two Guards would sit behind them in the sand.

No sooner had the chit-chat and commotion subsided than Rick, Roger, and Audra bowed in unison to their audience, and Roger managed to win instant corroboration from the audience to join him in humming and chanting an old-time circus introduction theme:

"Dit-dit-ditta, da-da, dut-dut-datta… dit-dit-ditta, da-da, dut-dut-datta… dit-ditta-dah! dit-ditta-dah! Dah-dah-dah-dah-dah-dah, dah dah, dah…dit-dit-ditta…

☙❧

Then all of that, embellished by knee-slapping, as they repeated the themed chant again and yet again,while Rick started doing flips and somersaults, handstands and kick-backs to a standing position. He then repeated the whole performance to a point of leaping onto a major strong-and-healthy-looking hanging vine that bound two palm trees together.

Swinging from that vine to other vines, he managed to simultaneously swing his macheté to cut off and grab pineapples and coconuts along the way, which he caught and lobbed gently to each of the three Guards.

While swinging between trees, he managed to catch a small parrot—which he carried while flying, himself, from vine-to-vine above the gathering—and delivered it to one of the two girlfriends who'd been tapping her feet to accompany his swinging motions between trees.

By this time, as she reached for the parrot, literally everyone was tapping their feet in the sand or clapping hands in rhythm to the chanting. Led by Roger's loud "La-la-la-la, la-la-la-la, la-la" singsong rhythm background throughout, and to Rick's seemingly impossible leaps and bounds above and around the gathering.

All of this activity captured everyone's attention to the extent that Audra was hardly noticed stringing rope between trees. Then, as she began to tightrope walk and literally dance, prompting heads to turn back and forth to try seeing everything happening at once, Roger maintained an undercurrent of rhythm sounds and bamboo stick-clicks throughout. Both performers moved in rhythm to Roger's clicking and hooting sounds.

At one point, Rick raced around the entire gathering alternating his running feet with his flips and vine-hanging swirls around them all, topped off by his one-on-one hand delivery in mid-flight of huge cut palm leaves, making sure each person got two leaves to keep their hands busy and away from firearms.

Throughout this entire forty-minute performance, Red Robbins successfully moved himself and his remaining six teammates deeper into the heavily-forested area leading to the back wall of the property and through a small back-end entrance, to spare them any lassoing and rope-climbing challenges.

Three of them proceeded quickly into the living quarters searching for the cash, while Red and the other three, all fully armed, headed for the front entrance to block the "audience" from re-entering the building to be prepared for confrontation.

Robbins' three-man, cash-hunter-team went quickly through trunks, suitcases—where they also found and confiscated passports—weathered old wooden boxes, closet and cabinet areas, in each of the ten rooms, and a number of areas that appeared to be freshly-dug into the ground in three of those rooms.

They took turns standing guard while the others searched and dug quickly and exhaustingly in seven of the ten rooms before getting tipped off by a tiny penknife blade stuck into the dried mud and corner next to what must have been the master bedroom curtained closet.

Jiggling their folding shovel into the corner, they uncovered a half-a-dozen short wooden planks under the mud floor and, just as they were about to tear off the top planks, an echoing gunshot rang out from the front performance area.

The three of them, guns loaded, raced to the front entrance. Then they quickly ducked back inside unnoticed when they realized that the shot was one of the Guards killing a gigantic rattlesnake everyone was looking at. The snake apparently threatened the end of the performance because Rick was grinning as he explained:

"Dis snake was not parda my act! HA! HA! . . . so, gracias mi amigos and now en este momento por mi finalmente my grand finale!"

Once the dead snake was moved off to the side, they all returned to their seats. The cash-hunters returned to rushing their digging to pull back the floor planks, and discovering a huge stash of U.S. cash.

The moment they saw the many hundreds of four-inch-thick packets of thousand-dollar bills, and realized the floor planks in one of the other two rooms was no doubt hiding the rest of the cash, they quickly grabbed their guns and hand-signaled thumbs-up to Robbins and the other two teammates through the open window they earlier all agreed to watch for that signal.

Rick had just introduced and entered into his grand finale with an amazing display of speed, strength, and creativity flying through the treetops, juggling coconuts, and somersaulting into a small sand dune next to his audience.

As everyone stood and began to applaud Rick's and Audra's performances, Roger's seven-member, fully-armed Support Team came quickly and startlingly toward the smiling audience-member Guards —whose clapping hands and armfuls of coconuts, pineapples and palm leaves left them at the mercy of the seven armed Support Team members. They arrived from seemingly out-of-nowhere from all sides, with guns drawn, and pockets full of handcuffs, and instantly commandeered the gathering by moving into Charlton and Gator's personal space, and quickly forcing weapons to be dropped and hands raised.

With guns aimed at them from just inches away, Charlton and Gator were promptly handcuffed, plus Charlton's right ankle was cuffed with Gator's left ankle, then each of them was handcuffed to neighboring palm tree roots and fittingly forced to lie face-down in the sand on each side of the dead rattlesnake.

And, as a safety measure, rifles were quickly provided to Rick and Roger, who thought nothing of shoving their weapons into culprit Gator and Charlton's crotches with every attempt that either culprit would make to talk.

All of this as Red and his team quickly and simultaneously disarmed the three Guards, cuffed them all—along with the two girlfriends and the cook—behind their backs and led the six of them carefully and very pleasantly into the building's front entrance, requesting them to sit quietly.

Rick and Roger told the cook and three Guards that as long as they cooperated fully, they would all be released as soon as the rest of the American Team worked it's way through the building, searching for legal American property that was stolen by Gator and Charlton. Both of them then introduced their Boss, Red Robbins.

With the help of Rick and Roger's limited language interpreting skills, Robbins explained that their Team was there to help them. He explained, "Only interest was in capturing Charlton and Gator and the American property they had stolen and that all of you will be released in uno momento with individual, personal mucho grandioso! recompense for each of you tres Guards y cocinero, which had been decided by both the United States and Costa Rican Governments working together. And you will be given all the details of what this is all about. It will be carefully reviewed with you quattro—thumb tucked in, he shows his four open-fingered hand—in cinco—he shows his five open-fingered hand—minutos!

The girlfriends were told, in front of the Guards, that the decision to release each of them would be up to the three Guards once the American Team departs with Charlton and Gator, who would be taken back to the United States to stand trial.

They were further informed that the cost of their travel back to where each came from would be paid for—but only for the next coming week—with special cards that the Guards would be given if either or both of them decide to return to their original homes where they lived before moving here.

"If the girlfriends choose to remain here and only with approval of the three Guards and the cook—the travel cards can be converted to help cover food and boat expenses. The tres Guards and cook would make that decision."

They explained that the American Team had been commanded to recover this stolen American property before turning property ownership including the boats plus some big amounts of American cash over to each of YOU. Not to worry.No Problemo! All is Bueno!

They were promised that they would get their guns back, that they would definitely be happy with their rewards.

And they did, and they were.

Chapter 47

Upbeat Rewards and Earned Returns

Clearly, Robbins' Team had taken total control, and led the cook and three native Guards into the large fortress living room space, to explain that while each had been getting paid $1 U.S. a week, they would each now be rewarded with $250 U.S. currency worth $25,000 each in Costa Rican dollars!

PLUS: Each of the four of them were informed of their sudden Costa Rican Government—signed, sealed, and delivered—shared twenty-five percent each ownership of the property, the building, all building furnishings and contents, plus the exterior wall, and all boats and motors, and the dock! PLUS the one acre of land that surrounds it all, donated by the C.R. Government. One more plus for them to share was an additional circular surrounding acre which overlaps a small part of the 850,000-acre Costa Rican Rain Forest, which was donated by the Costa Rican Government.

All of the ownership arrangements and official paperwork was signed by the Costa Rican President, as arranged via the California

Governor's office and facilitated by Professor Maddigan via his Language Arts Faculty Counterpart, Professor José Sánchez at Seaport County Community College and Professor Sanchez's uncle who's expected to run in the next C.R. Presidential Election.

Robbins made sure that everything was carefully explained, signed and verified for the new tax-free Costa Rican landowners.

Once all the rooms were double-checked and all U.S. cash and personal belongings of Gator and Charlton were removed, the three Guards were given their unloaded firearms back, along with a large box of ammunition to be left where the U.S. Jeeps were parked, they were then freed along with the cook, to decide among themselves how best to divvy up the newly-designated tax-free property ownership and all proceeds.

All legal documents, explained Robbins, would be duplicated and filed, including the signed versions, with both the U.S. and Costa Rican governments.

In just a matter of minutes, arrangements had been made and were announced to cover all moving expenses within Costa Rica for the two native girlfriends and amidst what appeared to be their artificial tears, the Guards monitored their suitcase-packing and arranged via the Senior Guard to have them, and their belongings, picked up by boat at high tide and taken to the coastal destination of Flocking Way and No Flocking Way to be set free.

The girlfriends' short-lived Travel Cards were promptly converted to an additional $250 U.S. to be divided equally between the cook and three Guards.

Returning to the Jeeps was a slow and deliberate process which included run-ins with an angry aggressive panther and two more threatening rattlesnakes...plus dozens of friendly monkeys. Charlton and Gator traveled chained to the back seats in separate Jeeps. Each was also securely-fastened with short, heavy-duty chains locked to the rear bumpers and to metal floor hoops to limit their movement in the vehicles.

All U.S. Team Members were enormously relieved and quick to ditch their all-black head-to-foot outfits, yielding to shorts, T-shirts and military baseball caps, saving their dress uniforms for the flight home.

On the trek back through the jungle, Robbins' Team Members took turns napping and even actually feeding the still cuffed bad guys their "No Talking" meals to avoid any utensil misuse.

The nine-officer team and two captives continued the rest of their return to civilization through endless mud, humidity and heat, animal and poisonous snake threats, nonstop insect bites, and scattered poison-ivy itching, along with chattery vine-swinging chimps, distant passing panthers, howler monkeys, purposefully side-tracked crocodiles, and swarms of spiders and mosquitos.

Robbins drove the last of the three Jeeps, but instead of having a chained-up prisoner like the other two in front of him, Robbins' Jeep had the cash chained to the back seat and metal floor hoops, and also carried Officers Focazio and Infusino. The lead Jeep carried one extra rotating officer.

Repeated Ham Radio call update messages were sent and relayed back to The States during their return travels to an awaiting private jet that departed for Newark Airport within an hour of having transferred officers, captives, equipment and three unidentified beat-up, heavy old suitcases.

The three Jeeps and ownership papers were turned over to Costa Rican government law enforcement teams.

Happily, the entire journey was officially registered and reported as uneventful except for Rick's diversionary circus performance, which Roger and Randy agreed they wanted to nominate for an Oscar because his performance literally saved their lives and enabled both the capture of Gator and Charlton, who were both delivered directly to a New Jersey State Prison Warden who immediately put them into Solitary Confinement.

THE TIDE TURNS

The stolen cash was delivered immediately to the heavily-guarded Seaport County FBI Vault for counting, verification, and processing in preparation of finally being able to return to the many hundreds of innocent victims throughout the County and the State!

Chapter 48

A Decision or Two and Clinking Glasses

Back Home

As Introductions"and Toasts were offered, the following individuals stepped forward: Police Chief John Oleson, Police Lieutenant Douglas Axel, and FBI Agent Randy "Red" Robbins—along with his eight-Military Officer Team Members including former military and current police Officers Ron Focazio and Mike Infusino, and The Performers: Officers Rick Alps, Roger Ringland, and Audra Kelly, plus their entire Recovery Mission Support Team of three police lab and travel technicians. All were honored with county media, and County business product and service donations at a Seaport County testimonial support and ceremony dinner on the Seaport County Community College Campus for returning with the two thieves, $11,875,000 in cash, and the entire Team of skilled officers all with no reported injuries.

The faculty and student Dining Hall was dressed-up for the occasion with student and faculty-created Costa Rican jungle music and art exhibits.

Professor Maddigan and JP and "Rico-as-in-Puerto" flown in for the occasion, were the featured guests and given a standing toast by all invited and special guests, including the New Jersey Governor, a U.S. Army General, a U.S. Navy Admiral, and top Washington D.C. officers from the U.S. Marine Corps, U.S. Air Force, and a special representative of California's new Governor.

All the guests had kind things to say about the two-man capture and money-recovery process, the success of the nine-member military and police team and leadership, and the plans for needy-family cash distribution.

All present also gave nonstop accolades to the groundbreaking plans for the new Student Communications Center. And Axe was rewarded a $5,000 Seaport County check for all that he did to help coordinate the Recovery Mission activities and help offset his low retirement income.

If there was a star of the evening to accompany the glitter of the New Jersey Governor's presence, it had to be "Rico as in Puerto" who was grinning ear-to-ear all night with appreciation for his cash and his all-expenses-paid surprise week at a New Jersey ocean resort in the United States, before his paid return to Costa Rica.

He brought the roof down with applause with his single sentence thank you comment when he was handed the two-thousand-dollar check, and Professor Maddigan stepped forward to inform the gathering of Rico's inability to pronounce the letter "T" just before Rico stepped forward and bowed to the hundreds of attendees as he said:

"Dank you for giving me da drip here and for da doo-dousand dollars reward check, dank you! Id means a gread deal doo me!"

❧❦

JP and Maddigan chat at dinner the next night,"Y'know what,

Professor? The last time I was here at the Oceanfront Steakhouse was the night we got back home from our summer vacation chase and you fell asleep early, and I took my old friend Katie Didde to dinner. " He nods that he remembers that night.

"In fact, "she adds, "we sat here at this very same table. Anyway, I got to a point of considering 'bout once a couple more semesters are over and I was actually thinking that night, thinking about a totally different place to go, but with all the things we most liked about our travels you and me. It was good to see her again and after sharing and comparing so many of the experiences we had, and that she had, and places we went, and that she went, and listening to Katie's travel experiences, and thinking all this time since then about where on Earth we might ever travel to next, and I've actually come up with—"

Maddigan interrupts to finish her sentence with a question mark. "A decision?"

JP continue. "Yes, well, I'm not sure it's a decision so-to-speak. Actually, it's more like a recommendation, like, uh, something to consider. Actually I mean I wouldn't want you thinkin' I'd ever make a decision like this alone, so it's just a suggestion, but —"

Maddigan interrupts: "Uh, can you just get to the point, JP?"

She takes a deep breath, hands him a tour guide book: "The Galapagos."

"Galapagos? As in Darwin's Theory of Evolution GALAPAGOS?"

"Absolute, she responds, as in your favorite brand of vodka!"

"You can't be serious, JP. What's with that? Why would we want to go there?"

"Funny you should ask, but you may want to sit back and order a drink and listen while I give you the answer!"

"Sounds like a plan," he says, as he gestures to the waiter. He orders a glass of Merlot. She orders a glass of Chardonnay.

"Y'know," he says, "only red wine has true anti-oxidant values?

She responds, "Yes, Professor, except for Chardonnay." They both grin and nod as they recall the same comments on their flight home to Newark Airport.

JP can't wait for the waiter to return, and, so, starts in. "A chain of nineteen fearless and curious wildlife islands we would get to by private yacht, after flying there from Nicaragua. The yacht has ten first-class bed-and-bath cabins that take up to twenty passengers. The yacht includes a full-time top-notch Physician, a Master Chef and Baker, a twenty-year experienced Captain and a crew of twenty-four including Galapagos Islands Guides. All are natives from the Galapagos or Nicaragua and almost all speak both English and Latino Spanish." She stops to take a quick breath, then continues.

"Katie Didde says the roof of the yacht has a bar with lounge chairs, and there's a hot tub for up to ten on the bow, a dining room, and a below-deck classroom for daily before-dinner prepping and reviewing of Galapagos history over a glass of wine, with Q&A highlights of each day's events and next-day island visit plans."

She stops talking long enough to thank the waiter who just brought their glasses of wine. They toast each other and take a sip before JP then picks up the momentum with Maddigan's clear and genuine interest.

"So, the Galapagos are home to over 300 species of reptiles, from friendly Iguanas and giant, hundred-year-old tortoises, to the world's only blue-footed-boobies—like big ducks that walk on their two big blue duck feet and come right up to visitors, and in fact, may even put their extra-large blue duck feet right on top of your shoes or sandals until you acknowledge them. The Galapagos even has seals you have to step over on the beach Oh! And penguins that waddle past you in every direction.

"And," she continues, "sharks they say are safe enough to be able to swim with!" She takes a quick breath and continues. "The yacht has three crew-operated motor, and picnic launches with different islands each day!" The launches take passengers back and forth to the nineteen islands for walks, hikes, and swims.

They each take a sip, but JP gulps hers; she doesn't want to slow down the moment-um of what she's saying, for fear of not getting everything in that she wants to say.

"And, by the way, passengers with boating experience, like us, are often invited into the control room to chat with the Captain during between-island travels. As for what to bring, Katie says we'd only need hats/bathing suits/windbreakers/shirts/shorts/jeans/ sneakers/sunglasses/a camera and binoculars... and we'd..."

"Hold it right there, young lady! What EVER would make you think I'd not be ready to start packing tomorrow? Sounds great! When do we leave?"

"Well . . ." (She turns on her bashful, chin-in/eyes wide open, face and responds): "Well, maybe as soon as we, uh...(long pause sip of wine) get married?. . . like, uh, maybe for a honeymoon? And maybe NOT with Flocky, Bollen, my family, Katie, Axe, Rico or other friends."

"So, let me get this straight, JP: I book the wedding and our two-week honeymoon tomorrow for in-between our next two semesters! And, see if I can arrange for Bollen to dog-sit Flocky?" Ear-to-ear grins. He nods assertively. They both laugh, hug, and kiss. "Oh, Rick, I love you soooo much!"

"Well, since I'm older than you, that goes double for me, JP!" They kiss and clink their wine glasses, then hug and kiss again! And if we don't spend too much, maybe we'll have enough to think about a new boat?" "Absolute!" she responds.

"Oh, by the way," he adds, "Uh, Will you marry me?" She nearly chokes on her last sip as she nods her head and says "Yup!" They kiss. Both laugh. Both keep hugging.

☙❧

"Uh, anything special you think we might need to know about

Low Tide in the Galapagos?" she asks, as they take a break, and push back from one another, yet are never distracted. "Yeah, don't do any drug deals that require waiting for High Tide to come around!... just kiddin, JP. All we really need to know about any LOW tide, anywhere, is that it's a one and only experience. A low tide can never be repeated because different shells and shifting sands make it unique. He takes a sip of wine.

. . . so, he continues: BOTTOM LINE for every Low Tide is that: NOW is the ONLY time and . . . that time and tide wait for no one . . . OR, as my grandfather used to say all the time ---and that, by the way, and I haven't told you this yet:

I just found out today that I've successfully convinced the powers that be at the College to inscribe my Grandpa Maddigan's favorite expression-- (He never knew the source, but he used to say it all the time!) across the entrance wall of the new Seaport County Community College Communications Center:

"NOW is the only time. The Past is over. The Future's not yet here."

THE END

ꙮ

A Factual Note of Interest

The Republic of Costa Rica was once known as Central America's most stable democracy. Costa Rica boasted the subcontinent's highest standard of living, and its complete demilitarization was a model for the world. Costa Rica is again a democracy, still a rarity in Central America.

Though its people are much poorer than they once were, they remain fully committed to their nation. And although the great powers that now compete for influence in Central America are different than during the Cold War, Costa Rica tries to maintain its traditional role as a neutral player in the region.

About the Author

Hal Alpiar is a native New Yorker and presently resides in New Jersey.

THE TIDE TURNS is the sequel to his first novel, *High Tide.* Over the years, Hal spent long periods of time vacationing in Costa Rica, which influences his stories. The following commentary reveals interesting information about Costa Rica.

The Republic of Costa Rica was once known as Central America's most stable democracy. Costa Rica boasted the subcontinent's highest standard of living, and its complete demilitarization was a model for the world. Costa Rica is again a democracy, still a rarity in Central America.

Though its people are much poorer than they once were, they remain fully committed to their nation. And although the great powers that now compete for influence in Central America are different than during the Cold War, Costa Rica tries to maintain its traditional role as a neutral player in the region.

During more than forty years in his working life, Hal authored more than five hundred magazine and newspaper feature articles, five hundred customized management training programs, seven hundred feature radio broadcasts, and over fifteen hundred online blog and guest blog posts.

A nationally-recognized business and professional practice development coach/consultant, Hal Alpiar brings over forty years of record client sales and patient volume, plus 25,000 training participants to the table.

A national award-winning marketer and a national book award-winning author, Hal draws from experience with his two 2-year term federal appointments to the SBA (U.S. Small Business Administration) Regional Advisory Council, his five years' service to the public affairs team of the NCQHC (National Committee for Quality Healthcare, now National Quality Forum)...and his frontline assistance with more than 500 successful business and healthcare practice startups and expansions.

The author of nine books, 100 websites, and 2,600 blogposts, Hal created and hosted his own daily feature radio show broadcasts for three years. Editor-in-Chief for three separate business publications, he was voted "Professor-of-the-Year" at both Pace University (NY) and Ocean County College (NJ), and served as a Special Instructor for the US ARMY.